THE BRANDANE CONNECTION

An Alison Cameron novella

MYRA DUFFY

www.myraduffywriter.com

British Library C.I.P.
A CIP catalogue record for this title is available from the British Library.

For Margaret and for Tamar, with memories of L.A.

PROLOGUE

This was a journey she'd never expected to make. Sure, Kate, her mom, had occasionally talked about Scotland, even mentioned Bute, but in a vague kind of way, whenever Jenna showed curiosity about her early life.

She hadn't been interested enough to ask about relatives, to be honest, except when there was a Memories day at school. Then Mom had had difficulty finding photos – there were none of her childhood and Jenna had to make do with the few black and white snaps she'd found in the old box in the den. Mom didn't seem to remember who the people in the photos were. In the end Jenna made up a story about them, though the teacher said suspiciously, 'That woman looks too young to be your grandmother.'

Yet here she was, on the ferry from Wemyss Bay to Rothesay, tingling with excitement at what she might find. It seemed like a dream, and she had to shake herself from time to time to convince herself it was real. And remember how she'd had to pluck up courage to make the journey. She'd been no further from her home in Los Angeles than that trip to Vermont that Ulmer had insisted on for his nephew's wedding. And now she'd travelled half-way across the world.

She gazed around the passenger lounge: the man at the ticket booth had assured her the crossing would take no more than thirty-five minutes. Hardly time enough for a cup of coffee. Even had she wanted one, the ferry was crowded and the queue at the onboard café was long: she'd be lucky to be served before they reached Rothesay.

Oh, oh! There was that woman she'd met on the flight from Los Angeles, deep in discussion with a young woman. What was her name again? Alice? No, Alison, that was it. Alison Cameron. A pleasant enough woman and Jenna had enjoyed chatting to her on the long transatlantic flight, but right now she was too excited to settle to a conversation with anyone. Besides, there was only so much about yourself that you wanted to reveal to a stranger, kind though Alison had been.

Jenna gazed out of the large window beside her table. The crossing had been smooth, though she guessed it might be a different story in winter. Her mom had been fiercely critical of the Scottish weather when she had been persuaded to talk about her life before America. "One of the reasons I love California," she'd said. "I remember storms so severe the ferry couldn't cross to the mainland for days or if it did, you'd be tossed about like a cork on water." Jenna thought her mom might have been exaggerating – surely even in those days there must have been a regard for health and safety.

'We're about to pass Toward,' a voice beside her said. 'Can you see the lighthouse?'

She turned, startled by this interruption to her thoughts. A stocky middle-aged man, clad in a sombre suit of black, had come up beside her. 'Sorry,' he said. 'I'm on the lookout for dolphins. If you're lucky you can spot them. You have a great view from these windows.'

'Really?' Jenna said.

'Mmm…yes. A beautiful day for a crossing to a beautiful island,' he said. 'It's no wonder so many people with a connection to Bute ask to be buried here.'

'You've been here before?' Jenna didn't want to appear rude, but she'd no intention of engaging in anything other than the briefest of exchanges and certainly not in a conversation about death.

He grinned. 'I suppose you could say that.' Then he appeared to realise what he'd said and gave a throaty laugh, displaying prominent front teeth. 'I live on the island. I'm travelling with the hearse on the car deck.' He nodded over to the café. 'My colleague is queueing in the café. It's been a long day and it's not over yet.'

Jenna thought this an odd approach till, 'You're a funeral director?' she said, understanding dawning.

'Yes. I studied at the University in Edinburgh, had hopes of a career in Architecture but I took over the family business a while back when my dad had to retire.'

He stopped suddenly and leaned over to get a better view. 'Look, look, there's a dolphin. Can you see it?'

Jenna followed the direction of his gaze. 'Gosh, I didn't expect that,' she said as one dolphin after another leapt from the water, creating a little froth of foam on the surface of the firth. She wasn't particularly superstitious, but this must surely be a good omen for her trip to the island.

'Come around to the other side of the ferry – you'll have a better view from there.'

He was so insistent that Jenna stood up to follow him. She became aware the man was talking to her again. 'Are you on holiday?'

Grudgingly she turned away from watching the frolicking dolphins. 'What? Oh, yes, I'm on vacation.' Then, as he seemed so easy to chat to, she said, 'I'm trying to track down my relatives. I think I might be due an inheritance through my mom, who came from the island originally.'

'Oh, really? How interesting? Do you know where your mother lived?'

Jenna shook her head. 'It was impossible trying to trace the right place from the States, so I employed a local…what do you call them…someone who traces your ancestors. Yolanda Sperkin came highly recommended.'

'A genealogist,' the man said. 'What did she find out for you?'

'That's the strange thing,' Jenna said, frowning. 'She sent me an email saying she'd discovered something important, but I haven't heard from her in a while and she hasn't answered my calls. I know she's on the island – she lives there part of the year. I hope there might be a good reason she hasn't been in touch.'

The man was once more gazing out over the water, though the dolphins had disappeared, and Jenna couldn't see the expression on his face as he said, 'You'll love Bute: it's a great place for a holiday, and…'

But Jenna didn't hear the end of his comment as the announcement came over the loudspeaker. 'Would all passengers please return to their cars as quickly as possible…'

'I'd better hurry,' the man said, buttoning up his jacket. 'We're at the front and I don't want to delay the other cars. People can be strange about a hearse on the ferry. I don't see why, myself. Everyone has to die.'

Jenna gave a little shiver. Thank goodness this odd guy was leaving. She breathed a sigh of relief, glad to end this discussion. She wasn't good at fending off strangers and their questions, and she'd already said enough about why she was on her way to Bute.

If she hadn't discovered that diary among the notebooks, she'd never have contemplated this journey. But when clearing the house in Santa Monica after her mother died, the house her mother had lived in all her life, she'd found the diary in a dusty suitcase in the far corner of the garret, a suitcase long-forgotten.

At first she'd been about to throw it out: there were some things that were too personal to read without being overcome by waves of grief. Now she was glad she'd found the diary again and had read it. And when she did, it was too late to turn the clock back. Her mother's reluctance to speak about her earlier life, about her Scottish roots, became clear. Here in these scribblings from the past was the reason why she'd said so little. Jenna understood what had been kept hidden for so long, had been the cause of her mother's reluctance to speak of her youth. Jenna was on her way to Bute to unravel a family secret, a secret that might make her very rich indeed. Once she'd spoken to the genealogist, Yolanda Sperkin, she'd be able to discover the truth.

The notebook was safely secured in her purse, in the zip compartment. Surely it wouldn't be too difficult on a small island to follow up the email from Yolanda. Since her husband's firm had got into financial difficulties, they'd been pretty short of money in spite of her working two jobs. Not that it was Ulmer's fault that he'd gotten sick and that no-good manager had taken advantage of him. She sighed. But that was about to change, and once she'd found the place her mom described in the diary, had the proof provided by the genealogist, her inheritance would solve all their problems.

CHAPTER ONE

It seemed so simple when Susie suggested it. But that was always the way with whatever Susie planned. And as she was one of my closest friends, and had been for a long time, I found myself agreeing with her as usual.

'You can't possibly be in the U.S. and not come down to Los Angeles to visit me,' had been her immediate response when I told her I'd be coming over to Washington to see my husband, Simon, who was working there.

'I know geography isn't my strong point,' I replied, 'but surely Washington is a long distance from Los Angeles? I don't think I'd be able to fit it in. My plan is to have a short trip to the U.S.' Even as I spoke, I realised Susie wouldn't accept this as an excuse.

'Nonsense. All you have to do is hop on a plane and it'll take no more than a couple of hours. Everyone here travels by plane, the same way as you would use a bus or a train in Scotland. I'll sort out the arrangements for you.'

It would be good to see her: since she married Dwayne and went to live in America, I've missed her company and her support. It did seem foolish not to take advantage of being on the same continent. Goodness knew when I'd be back in the States.

My trip to Washington had been more successful than I could have hoped. After a lot of worry recently about my marriage, and the real reason Simon had taken up a contract in America, my time with him had eased my fears. Even better, he'd assured me that as soon as his work in Washington was finished, he'd be coming back to Scotland for good.

'Not immediately, Alison,' he'd warned me. 'There are still a few months of the contract to run, but I can do the final report at home, or most of it.' He stopped and gave a wide grin. 'And after that, I intend to retire.'

I wasn't sure what he meant by a "final report". As far as I knew he'd gone to Washington to take up a post as a trainer, given his long experience in education, but now wasn't the time to be asking difficult questions.

And his last comment both delighted and worried me. I couldn't believe he'd give up working: he's too restless to fall into a 'do very little' routine. I was still working – would he expect me to retire also? But that was in the future – for the moment everything seemed to be going smoothly. He was coming home, and my marriage concerns were over. And the silly idea I'd had that his post in Washington was of a secretive nature – well, silly was the word for it. He was on a perfectly ordinary training contract. Or so I persuaded myself. It was easier that way.

A week in the sunshine of California with Susie was a holiday to look forward to. She was right – my plane journey from Washington took no time, at least compared with the trip across the Atlantic from Scotland.

She picked me up at the airport and we drove over to her house in a suburb of L.A., chattering non-stop. 'Dwayne is so sorry he'll miss you, but he's at a

Credit Union conference in Las Vegas this week. He's chair of the local committee so has to be there. You'll guess they have a lot to talk about. There's still a huge gulf between the rich and the poor in this city.'

We pulled up in front of a single-storey whitewashed building, the neatly manicured front lawn surrounded by a profusion of giant cacti, many in bloom, crowded together as though jostling for position. Along the narrow pavements, large Jacaranda trees loomed bright against the cloudless blue sky, shedding their purple flowers to create drifts on the roadways.

'Messy things,' Susie said, 'spilling their flowers everywhere,' but I thought they looked pretty.

'Home, sweet home,' Susie said as we got out of the car. 'You can see it's like Bute,' and she pointed to the palm trees, swaying in the light breeze.

'It looks so attractive,' I said. 'But I think the palm trees are a bit bigger than those on Bute.' An understatement: they were indeed gigantic, each of the long thick trunks topped by a head of large palm leaves.

She grinned. 'This place is ideal for Dwayne and me,' as she popped a button on the dashboard to open the boot and retrieve my suitcase. 'Let's go inside. It's pretty hot this afternoon. We'll go down the side path to the yard and the back door.'

The yard turned out to be an extensive area, partly cultivated with raised vegetable beds, and in the far corner a swimming pool, glittering turquoise in the sunshine, took up the rest of the space. Beside the back porch an orange tree and a lemon tree bowed under the weight of the ripening fruit.

'You can have a dip later,' she said, noticing my eyes light up as I spied the pool. 'We use it a lot in the summer.'

Once we were settled in her huge open-plan living room with a cooling drink and the air-conditioning on, she said, 'And how is Bute? Have you been back there recently?'

I shook my head. 'No, my work lately has been Glasgow or Edinburgh based. I don't anticipate returning to the island soon.' I didn't say my decision was largely because every time I went there I seemed to become involved in a problem not of my making.

'Did you notice? Bute's been in the news recently,' she said.

I frowned. 'How?' Even in this short time in America I felt out of touch with what was happening back in Scotland.

She lifted the remote control for the giant TV dominating the far wall. 'We get BBC news,' she said, 'and there was a story yesterday. I recorded it for you. I thought you might have missed it.'

She flicked through several recorded programmes before stopping. 'Yes, here it is.'

It was a small item on the news, but the story was one I wasn't aware of. There had been a suspicious death at a worker's cottage on the estate of one of the large Victorian mansions that were a feature of the island. A woman had been found dead there a couple of days before. But there was no further information: not her name, nor the name of the property.

'Not a great deal that's newsworthy there,' I said, shrugging. What's more, it was of no concern to me, thankfully. 'And I won't be going to Bute any time soon.'

'I thought it might have been a bigger story back in Scotland?' I suspected that Susie, despite loving her life in L.A., was homesick from time to time and seized eagerly on any crumb of news.

'Sorry, Susie. I've heard nothing about the death of this poor woman.'

She looked disappointed, but though Bute has been part of my life for many years, it had been some time since my last visit. And I was in Los Angeles to see Susie and to have a holiday, not worry about incidents that didn't concern me.

The days flew past: Susie had arranged a full programme of activities for me, including visits to what she called 'the seaside' resorts of San Clemente and La Laguna. Lovely as these were, the vast distances we had to travel surprised me, though Susie seemed to have adapted well.

It seemed no time till Susie was dropping me off at LAX airport with the stern admonition, 'Now you've found your way, be sure to come back again soon.'

'I promise,' I said as I hugged her farewell and I meant it. We'd had such a good week, with lots of fun and laughter, reminiscing about our time teaching at Strathelder High School. I'd seen a lot of Los Angeles and its attractions, though the freeways I found unnerving. Thank goodness Susie was a confident driver.

But fate has a way of intervening...and often the best-laid plans go awry.

I anticipated a return to Glasgow to complete the final edit on my latest commission, before pitching for the next one. My holiday in the U.S. had given me plenty of material for several articles.

The last thing I expected was to find myself on the ferry back to the Isle of Bute.

CHAPTER TWO

The most interesting part of travelling on your own is that you never know who you'll meet. I've had plane journeys where the person beside me plugged into headphones and stared resolutely ahead for the entire journey. While I suspect, when in a charitable mood, that this is often no more than a fear of flying, I'm not the kind of person who can stand silence for long. But then, I've also had trips where my travelling companion has chattered non-stop, scarcely giving me the opportunity to say a word.

That was why, on this long trip back from L.A., I was delighted to find myself seated beside a woman who looked to be about my own age.

After I introduced myself she said in a quiet voice, 'I'm Jenna Pattersmain,' and it was immediately clear from her accent she wasn't Scottish or possibly hadn't lived in Scotland for a long time. A few minutes later I'd learned not only was she on her way to Glasgow, but she intended to continue her journey to the Isle of Bute.

'I know the island well,' I said.

'You're a native of the island?' She frowned. 'There's a special name for them, isn't there, people born on Bute?' She hesitated, then said with an air of triumph, 'A Brandane, that's it!'

'No,' I laughed. 'I'm not from the island. And how did you know someone born on Bute was called a Brandane? Especially as you're from the U.S?'

'No idea,' she muttered, 'I must have read it,' before adding quickly, 'I hope the weather isn't as bad as I've heard it can be.'

Why did she sound as if she was being evasive? And if she was, why lie about a simple answer to my question?

But now wasn't the time for being too inquisitive and instead I recounted various stories of my trips to the island, heavily edited, of course. I didn't want to alarm her, so I said little about the perilous situations I'd been involved in. But I did include several interesting anecdotes, as well as a little about the history and the geography of the island, and though I couldn't say she showed great enthusiasm, she listened politely enough, interrupting with the odd question.

It wasn't till I mentioned Susie Littlejohn and my holiday in L.A., that she suddenly perked up. 'That's my hometown,' she said. 'How did you like it?'

She didn't live anywhere near Susie, but she was intrigued by my account of the places I'd visited.

'I've not been to any of those: I guess when you're a visitor you make a lot more effort,' she grinned. 'I'll put some of them on my bucket list for when I get back. In the meantime you've given me plenty of ideas about where I can visit while on Bute.'

Gradually our conversation became more desultory and I fell asleep for a while, only waking abruptly as the voice of the pilot announced we'd soon be landing in Glasgow.

When we stepped down from the transit bus at the Glasgow airport terminal, I bid Jemma farewell, wished her a pleasant time on Bute and hurried out of the building to find a taxi. All I could think about was getting home as quickly as possible to catch up on some sleep.

I imagined this would be the last I saw of her, but how wrong can you be?

CHAPTER THREE

'I can't possibly!'

I sat across from Nora, my commissioning editor, in her office in Glasgow, unable to believe what she was saying.

Nora leaned back in her executive chair, almost as well-upholstered as she was. The light streaming in behind her from the large window of this office on the fourth floor of the building in St Vincent Street gave her light blonde hair the appearance of a halo. But she was no soft touch. A core of steel had propelled her at the age of thirty into a position as one of the most important editors in the country.

She tapped her fingers on the desk. 'Alison, this is a tricky situation. Baxter is ill, very ill, and he's not going to be able to finish the article he's supposed to be writing. I thought you'd be pleased at this offer.'

I ignored the last comment. 'Can't it wait till he's recovered?'

'No. This article is for one of our best clients, the American magazine *Across the Seas*.'

I knew the magazine well – I also knew how difficult it was to pitch to them and why Nora wouldn't want to have to tell them she couldn't fulfil the contract.

'Mmm…' I said, stalling for time.

'And there is a deadline. Which should suit you well, Alison. You're reliable at meeting deadlines. And if this one goes down well with readers, there may even be a follow-up series. That would be good, wouldn't it?'

This attempt at flattery didn't impress me. Nora had secured me several articles lately, mainly about Glasgow and I'd enjoyed doing them. Life as a freelance writer can be feast or famine and since I'd signed with Nora's agency, the work had been more regular. I didn't want to lose her as a source of a steady income.

She leaned across her massive desk. I think she has issues with status to be honest, or perhaps she likes to keep a good distance between herself and her writers.

'It's well-paid, extremely well-paid,' she said, before mentioning a figure that made me gasp in surprise. She smiled; no doubt convinced this was her trump card. 'So, it's agreed then? You'll do it.' A statement, not a question.

'You haven't told me what the article is about?'

'Oh, didn't I? It's a commission I'm sure will suit you well.' She flicked through a folder on her desk before saying, 'It's about Maria North or Stuart, the wife of the Marquess of Bute. Maria North was English, and the second Marquess of Bute supposedly built the village of Kerrycroy, modelled on an English village, to ease her homesickness.'

'And you want me to go to Bute to do the research.' This was what she was trying to come around to. I wasn't sure I was as pleased as Nora thought I'd be.

'Correct,' Nora said triumphantly. 'You've such a lot of experience of the island.' Seeing the frown on my face, she added hastily, 'And Baxter has left enough material to get you started. I'm sure it won't take you long.'

'I'm not certain that's accurate,' I replied, lest Nora thought this might be an excuse to cut my fee. 'I'd have to do the research, spend time in the archives at Mount Stuart.'

'Nonsense,' Nora said, 'Baxter's already been there. He's happy to let you have his notes.'

'I suppose that might help,' I said grudgingly, 'but there will still be a lot of work.' I'd met Baxter before, and I wasn't confident he was as diligent as Nora was trying to claim.

The article might take up most of my energies while on Bute, but on this occasion I was determined to build in a little leisure time. Right now the island would be at its best: sunny and warm – at least most days. And I wasn't going to let Nora think I might be easy to persuade.

'Of course, of course, Alison. I understand perfectly. But you've nothing else on right now, have you?'

You know I don't, I thought, but didn't say so. As I'd completed my last assignment as soon as I'd returned from America, and had no other work in view, I'd no excuse for refusing the commission on Maria North. And this would be a favour Nora owed me. What's more, she was right. I knew the island well and would be able to complete the article more quickly than other writers on her books.

And so, in late June, no more than a couple of weeks after returning from Los Angeles, I found myself packing my bags and heading once again for the Isle of Bute.

CHAPTER FOUR

As I boarded the MV Argyle ferry to Bute and climbed the stairs from the car deck to the passenger lounge, to my surprise I spied the woman I'd met on the plane from Los Angeles. She was sitting alone at one of the tables at the window, idly flicking through her phone. Jenna, that was her name. I was about to go over and join her – it would have been rude not to – but I was distracted by a voice saying, 'Back again, Alison?'

I turned to greet the speaker, but I didn't recognise the woman standing in front of me. Or, more accurately, I'd a vague memory of having met her before. But she could have been one of several people – an ex-pupil from my years as a schoolteacher at Strathelder High, or someone I'd met on one of my many trips to Bute.

'Hello,' I said, putting on a bright smile, hoping she would give me a clue.

'I can see you don't remember me,' she grinned. 'Penny, Penny Curtis. I was one of the archaeologists on the ill-fated dig at the house at Ettrick Bay some time ago.'

'Why, of course,' I said. She'd changed in the years since I'd last seen her. She'd put on a little weight and her long brown hair was now short, showing off her ears adorned by several stud earrings.

'I'm not surprised if you've tried to forget it,' she said. 'I've attempted to erase it from my memory. It was a terrible time for all of us.'

'And what are you doing on the island? Another dig?'

She laughed and pointed to a group of young people in the far corner of the ferry. 'No, I'm in the world of academia now. I'm lecturing at the University of Aberdeen and my colleague and I have brought a group of students to the island for a field trip. Bute has some of the most interesting Bronze Age remains in Scotland.'

We chatted for a few minutes, before she said, 'I'd better go back to my charges. They may be adults, but occasionally they seem to be more work than children. I might see you on the island.'

As she walked over to join an increasingly boisterous group, I thought how I didn't envy her. While a lot of my time as a teacher at Strathelder High had been enjoyable – and even rewarding – I didn't miss it. But Penny seemed happy with her new career and her students.

I scanned the lounge for a sight of Jenna, but she was deep in conversation with a young man in a black suit which looked far too heavy for the warm weather. Something in the water had caught their interest, judging by the way they were peering intently out of the window. No matter. I'd catch up with her later, when we returned to the car deck.

There was no sign of her as I made my way downstairs to claim my car, in obedience to the voice from the loudspeaker, but then I was sure to meet her on the island. Even with the local population of six thousand swelled by summer visitors, it was difficult not to bump into people you knew.

I'd decided to use a small hotel, The Ferry Rest, near Kerrycroy as my base: I'd be spending most of the week there and even with the help of Baxter's notes, I'd have to factor in research time at Mount Stuart. The hotel been recommended by a family friend, but it wasn't a part of the island I knew well.

I was worried about the article I'd agreed to write. While I'd a fair degree of familiarity with the story of the Stuarts, had written about them before and had visited Mount Stuart House on a number of occasions, I'd little material on Maria North. There was a lot to do in a short time. As well as researching the details of her life, I wanted to get a feel for the village that meant so much to her. Once I'd had time to go through what Baxter had written, I'd a hunch there would be little of real value, no matter what Nora thought. A brief glance told me a lot of the material was of a general nature, or concerned with the second Marquess, rather than Maria, his first wife, so I was starting from a low base.

What's more, my time was limited: foolishly, I'd agreed I could complete the assignment in a week, realising Nora was under a lot of pressure. A decision I was now regretting as I began unpacking my case in a large room which would be my home for the duration of my stay. The room, with an exceptional view of the bay, was comfortable enough, decorated in restful shades of blue and cream. There was the bonus of a proper desk in the alcove but, even so, I could see my hopes of a few days' holiday rapidly disappearing.

There was a knock on the door and the owner, Izzie Mace, put her head round the door. 'Everything okay? You'll let me know if you need anything else?'

'Fine, thanks. It's so comfortable.'

Izzie smiled. 'I've heard a lot about you,' she said before closing the door behind her.

I sighed. Why should I not be surprised? Many of my visits to the island had involved trouble and news spreads quickly. I set up my laptop and sat down. No time like the present. Perhaps I could begin with the title of the piece? Or even write the introduction? But inspiration eluded me, and I fell back to gazing out of the window.

It was a beautiful evening, the sun going down across the bay in a riot of pink and purple. The ferry was gliding towards its destination of Wemyss Bay, a trio of seagulls diving and swooping above it. Even with the pressure of a deadline, surely a week here in the peace of the island would be an opportunity to relax after my hectic time in the United States.

And I could look forward to Simon's return to Scotland before Christmas – this time for good.

Everything was going according to plan, though a little niggle of doubt crept in as I remembered previous trips to Bute, but I dismissed these concerns as no more than the result of tiredness after my journey. I was an experienced writer, and all would be well.

CHAPTER FIVE

How wrong can you be? Delivering this article to Nora on time would be a lot more difficult than I'd imagined – and it was nothing to do with the scantiness of Baxter's notes.

I'd no option but to make an early start, because my first task, before I could write a word, was to go into Rothesay. As I'd opened my computer just before going to bed the previous night, thinking it would be a good idea to answer my emails, there had been a sudden flash and then an *Error* message appeared on the screen in bright red capital letters.

Several reboots later, there was no improvement and panic began to set in, especially as I hadn't backed up the research I'd done on Maria North before leaving Glasgow. It wasn't extensive, but it was a start. How stupid was that! And I was supposed to be a professional writer.

A quick word with Izzie Mace and I was directed to a computer repair shop in the town: as soon as I thought they might be open for business, I set off.

The shop, *Speedy Computer Repairs,* was on the far side of Rothesay, between a Zavaroni's Ice Cream shop and a charity shop and, after several attempts, I managed to squeeze into a parking space on Argyle Street. As I crossed the road, my one thought was, what if I was told my computer was beyond repair? There was the possibility I could write the article longhand and type it up once back in Glasgow, but there might be the small problem of not being able to read my writing. Years of using a computer had impacted on the quality of my handwriting skills.

The young man in *Speedy Computer Repairs* wore a badge proclaiming himself to be 'Tyler: Computer consultant' but he looked far too young to be a consultant. The most noticeable thing about him was his bright red hair, gelled into spikes, almost a work of art.

He wrinkled his nose as he plugged in my laptop. 'How old is this machine?'

'Six years,' I hazarded, trying to remember when I'd bought it.

He shook his head as though in sorrow. 'It means you can add on a couple of years. It's like when people are asked how much they drink – they always underestimate.'

I didn't think it was quite the same, but he was the expert and my laptop needed attention quickly. I didn't want to upset him by contradicting him.

He lifted the laptop up and looked underneath. 'It's pretty old for a computer – technology has moved on…'

'Yes, yes, it's my intention to buy a new one as soon as I'm home,' I said, having made no such decision. 'But can you do anything with this one. I need it urgently.'

He sighed, then pressed the Start button and the machine whirred into action. 'Dear, oh, dear. Have you been defragmenting it regularly?'

Or rather, I think that's what he said. I held my breath. Perhaps I'd made a mistake, and there was nothing wrong with the computer. But no, a few seconds later the same error message flashed up on the screen.

'Give me a couple of hours,' he said, shaking his head again. 'I'm in the middle of finishing an update for another customer.' He gestured round the shop, where computers sat on shelves in a haphazard fashion. 'I'm on my own here for the moment. Jill is off on holiday for a few days. We're not usually busy at this time of the year. I can't understand it.' He said this in an accusing voice, which I ignored.

He must have noticed the worried look on my face, because suddenly he grinned, saying, 'Don't worry, I've rescued much worse than this.'

He gestured to a small seating area beside the door at the front of the shop but preferring not to wait around in case he chided me further about neglecting to defragment my computer, I made my escape. 'I'll walk along to Helmi's and have a coffee,' I said, 'and come back later this afternoon.' Being Bute I knew I could safely be away for a while, no matter how speedy Tyler claimed to be. One of the best things about the island is the lack of urgency: problems are solved, but there's not the frantic pace of life in the city.

He grunted in reply, his attention focussed on the task in hand, then said as I reached the door, 'Give me a call first and I'll let you know what's happening.'

I closed the shop door behind me, unwilling to consider what I'd do if my computer was beyond repair. It would mean a trip back on the ferry, over to the nearest shopping centre in Greenock, meaning more time lost. And the expense of a new computer, which would wipe out most of the profit I'd make from the article.

But by now I was more than ready for a top-up of coffee and I hurried along the street to Helmi's Café, only stopping at Toffo's Newsagents in Guildford Square to buy a copy of the latest edition of the local paper. Coffee and a sugary pastry would surely revive me. In my haste to reach the computer shop as quickly as possible, I'd had a meagre breakfast.

Helmi's had just opened and I was the first customer. The pink and grey décor, the French style furniture and the tempting array of cakes on display immediately lifted my spirits. Time to relax here for a while, forget about my computer.

I opted for a seat beside the window, looking out over the Albert Pier and the Ferry Terminal beyond, watching the MV Bute glide through the water towards its berth. While I waited for my order to be delivered, I spread the local paper out on the table. The front page was entirely taken up by the death Susie had talked about, but this time there was an update. This death had been no accident – it was being treated as murder and there was a police appeal for information.

Before I could finish reading about this disturbing development, my attention was caught by a figure walking slowly past the café, head bowed. It was Jenna. I rapped loudly on the window and for a moment I thought she didn't see me, but suddenly she looked up and a look of recognition dawned.

I gestured to her to join me and she hesitated, as though trying to decide, before pushing open the door and coming over to sit down opposite me.

'How are you?' I said. 'I saw you on the ferry, but I met someone I hadn't seen for a long time and didn't have the chance to speak to you.'

She waved away the waiter as he came over to take her order.

'Okay, I guess,' she said, but there was a catch in her voice. She gazed down at the table and began to fiddle with the menu.

'Are you enjoying your holiday?' I said, unwilling to sit in silence.

'I'm not on holiday,' she said, a note of anger creeping into her voice. 'And nothing is going according to plan.'

Suddenly she noticed the copy of the newspaper on the table. She jabbed at the headline. 'It's such a muddle. And now this.'

'This death? Surely this isn't to do with you, any concern of yours?'

She stared at me. 'Of course it is. And I don't know what I'm going to do.'

Then, to my horror, she put her head in her hands and began to sob loudly.

CHAPTER SIX

When she'd recovered a little, Jenna's story was a strange one. Persuaded finally that a cup of coffee would be a good idea, she'd also succumbed to the temptation of one of Helmi's cakes.

'It started when Mom died a couple of years since,' she said, choking back a sob, then pausing to take a sip of coffee. 'She'd been ill for a long time and she was always secretive about her past. All we knew was that she came from Scotland, but apart from a few photos she had we learned little about her early life, and nothing about possible relatives we might have here.'

'Very odd,' I said. 'In most cases people are eager to let their families know where they originated from.'

'You'd think so, but when you asked her, she'd give an evasive reply and, to be honest, as kids we weren't interested in the past.'

'As none of us were at then,' I murmured, as she paused again. She was clearly finding this memory difficult. 'Take your time.'

Jenna pulled out a pack of tissues from her bag and wiped her eyes. 'After she died and we were clearing her house, we found some notebooks. She'd hidden them in a box at the back of the garret. At first they seemed of little interest.' Jenna bit into her cake, then drained her cup of coffee.

I waited, impatient for her to continue, but afraid she'd stop if I broke in. And it was clear she was anxious to tell someone. Now I'd invited her to join me, I had to hear the rest of the story.

'In the stress of sorting out her stuff – and there was a lot of it – the notebooks were kind of overlooked. The friend who helped with the clearing insisted I keep them, go through them at some point, but I didn't get around to it.' She shrugged, seemingly having recovered her poise. 'You know how it is. Work, family commitments and life in general get in the way. I took them, but they went into the basement together with the other stuff I couldn't bear to part with.'

She gazed out of the window as though gathering her thoughts. 'Then, last year, my husband, Ulmer, and I decided to downsize. The kids had left home and we didn't need so much space. And my husband's business was in trouble – no one wanted to buy what he was selling. He'd had a spell of bad health and we found out his manager had been less than honest with the accounts.'

I wondered what might be behind this disclosure, but I didn't want to interrupt to ask questions about her husband.

'And that's when you found the notebooks again?' I prompted her, sneaking a look at my watch. My computer might be ready by now and I was anxious to phone to check on progress, knowing if it couldn't be repaired I'd have to go over to Greenock.

'Yep. I'd forgotten about them, but for some reason, I decided one night to have a quick look through them, see if there was anything worth keeping. And that's when I remembered one of the notebooks was a kind of diary she'd kept off and on since coming to America.' There was a moment's hesitation as she fiddled with one of the paper napkins lying on the table, folding and refolding it. 'And when I discovered the man I thought was my pop wasn't. Mom had been married before and had come to the States from this Isle of Bute.' She stopped again, as though the memory was still raw. 'I couldn't believe it at first, thought it must be a mistake. Then when I'd had time to think about it, what could I do but try to find out the truth. It sure explained a lot – the secrecy, the lack of photos, Mom's reluctance to talk about her past.'

'And your father's name? You found what it was?'

She made a face. 'According to Mom's notebooks, his name was Foster, but I don't know if that was his real name. Mom described the house they lived in on Bute – it sounded like a mansion, with land around it. A huge estate.'

This might have been an exaggeration, I thought, as there were many large Victorian mansions on the island, but from what I knew most of them had large gardens rather than lands that could be called an estate. Despite my reservations about becoming involved, I was beginning to feel sorry for Jenna, though it seemed foolhardy of her to travel all the way to Bute to find her father on the evidence of flimsy details in an old notebook.

'How far have you managed to get?' I asked. 'Have you tracked down the family?'

She pointed to the local paper. 'I got a contact through a genealogist back home, found a woman who lived on the island, who said she could help me. It was a woman called Yolanda Sperkin and she had a good reputation for this kind of work, and I got in touch with her, but...'She broke off and I realised with a sudden feeling of horror what she was trying to tell me.

Picking up the copy of the newspaper, I pointed to the front page.

'You mean this woman, the one who they now say was murdered, was the genealogist you'd hired to trace your mother's family?'

She nodded. 'I can't work it out. Why should anyone want to kill her? She'd emailed me, said she'd found something of great interest to me and promised she'd send on more information. But she didn't follow up her email and then, when I discovered what had happened, I couldn't let it alone. I had to find out for myself.'

The death of Yolanda Sperkin was odd, but it wasn't necessarily anything to do with Jenna, nor with her attempts to find her family. Who knew what might have been going on in her private life. 'What have you managed to discover so far?'

'I was so certain I knew where the house was. Looks like Mom didn't intend the diary should be read, but in the end she died so suddenly I guess she didn't have time to get rid of it. But I've no idea why she didn't tell me about all this.'

I should have left her story there: instead I prompted her, 'And?'

'I got a map of Bute from the Tourist Office...the one on the front..'

'The Discovery Centre?'

'That's the one. I checked out the details in the diary against the map and finally plucked up courage and went to the house I thought was the right one, but the guy who answered the door seemed mystified by my questions. He was kind but couldn't help. Couldn't even suggest what I might try next.'

'Are you positive you had the right place?'

Jenna reached down and pulled a small blue notebook from her bag, placing it between us on the table. 'Here's the diary – you can see for yourself.' She pushed it towards me.

I hesitated. If I opened this notebook, I might be committing myself to an involvement I didn't want. I thought about my laptop, hopefully sitting ready in the *Speedy Computer Repairs* shop. What I should do was make an excuse to Jenna and leave her to work on her search for her father.

Instead I lifted the notebook and begin to read. The computer – and my latest commission – could wait.

CHAPTER SEVEN

Jenna's mood brightened considerably as I began to flick through the diary, but whether this was because of my show of interest or the effect of Helmi's cake was debatable. What she passed to me was a small notebook, the kind you could buy in any shop and Jenna's mother had carefully noted dates, and on several occasions, times at the top of each entry. Some were short, others long and detailed, with most of the content a seeming collection of random thoughts about her impressions of life in America. Except for the unusually long entry at the beginning, giving details of the house on Bute she'd abandoned to flee to the States.

Even so, though the house and the location were described in detail, it could be one of many mansions on the island.

'There's too much info to take in right now,' I said, 'but I am willing to look at your mother's account of the house and help you try to identify it, if I can.'

'Take the diary with you,' Jenna said eagerly. 'I can't make sense of it. If I could get it wrong once, I could do so again. I thought it would be easy to find the house Mom described.' She sniffed, pulling a tissue from her bag to wipe her eyes.

'Look at this.' She leaned over and began to thumb quickly through several pages.

'It might be easier if you did it the right way up,' I said, pushing it towards her. She took the notebook from me and stopped at various pages before handing it back to me, pointing to a double entry, 'Look, this is the best description of the house I could find.' She stabbed half-way down the page. 'And this is the important bit.'

I scanned the entry: there were lots of details about the kind of house, but the location wasn't immediately evident. Little wonder Jenna had made a mistake, gone to the wrong house.

'What made you decide to go there? 'I asked.

She pulled a map out of her bag. 'As I said, when I arrived on the island I went straight to the Tourist Office in…what is it called again?'

'The Discovery Centre,' I said quickly, anxious for her to continue her story.

'Yep. That's it. I knew they'd have a proper map of Bute, much better than the one I could get from the internet.'

She spread the map out before me, taking up the whole table and I had to move swiftly to rescue my coffee cup as it threatened to slip off the edge.

'Look at the entry in the diary – it says the house is right next to the ferry crossing.'

'Maybe, but the description also says "…surrounded by estate lands," so it can't be near the ferry crossing from Rothesay to Wemyss Bay.'

She looked puzzled. 'But this was written a long time ago – I guessed the land round the house had been built up over the years.'

'Not likely. It's more probable your mother is talking about the other ferry crossing, a house near there.'

'There's more than one crossing? Where?'

'Yes, there's a short crossing at Rhubodach, taking you to Colintraive and the longer journey by road to Glasgow.'

'I didn't know.' She peered at the map. 'Show me.'

I pointed out the place on the map and she sat back, sighing. 'I guess I should've taken advice before haring off on a wild goose chase.'

'Give me a minute,' I said and there was silence as I scanned the pages with the details of the house where her mother had lived, my concentration broken by the distraction of the door to the café opening and a group of holidaymakers surging in, laughing loudly.

I looked up, trying to think through the consequences of what I'd read. 'It sounds as if it's a substantial property,' I admitted, 'and there aren't many large houses on the other side of the island. Most of the properties are farms, or cottages.'

She looked crestfallen. 'But surely my mom wouldn't have got it so wrong…or worse, lied? Why would she do that? She never intended this to be read, so there'd be no point in making it up.'

I hated to think Jenna was about to be disappointed, but it seemed foolish to make the long journey to Bute on the strength of a description in an old notebook. I knew too well how memory can play tricks. While many Americans are eager to find their roots, there was an intensity about Jenna's search, making me suspect there was something she wasn't telling me. And it was more than the usual interest in family history.

'What made you decide to track down your family, your father – or why now?'

She stared at me, as though weighing up what she should reveal. Then she flipped through several pages before stopping. 'There,' she said, jabbing with her finger. 'I don't think this needs explanation.'

I quickly scanned the entry she'd identified, the text heavily underlined. The writing wasn't that easy to read, as though it had been written in haste. Several times I had to stop to ask Jenna to decipher her mother's handwriting for me.

I read the entry twice before looking up in astonishment. 'Your mother owned this house you're looking for? Your mother and father didn't divorce?'

'Yep! That's right. And don't you see what it means?'

I did, but I wanted her to say it.

'It means I'm the rightful owner of this property on Bute. And what's more, I intend to claim it. That's the purpose of this trip, why I've invested time and money. If I find it, I'll sell it: it will solve all our money problems.'

'But it's only an entry in a diary. I'm not sure this would be of any legal standing.'

She frowned, then reached into her bag again to pull out a yellowing sheet of paper. 'This agreement was signed by my mom and the man I now believe was my dad. He was allowed to live in the house – I guess she felt guilty about abandoning him.'

This piece of paper didn't change anything as far as I could see. Yes, it was an agreement of sorts, but it wasn't witnessed and there was no date on it and I gave it back to her without comment.

I listened in silence as, bit by bit, Jenna recounted the story of her financial difficulties. How her husband had been cheated, how his illness meant he'd had to let go the business he'd worked so hard to build up. 'Even when we sold up, bought a tiny apartment, there wasn't enough to clear the debts.'

So here it was at last, the true reason for Jenna's trip. While I now understood, or thought I did, there was one question troubling me. How accurate was the diary? The entry claiming she'd once owned the house might be true, or it might be no more than a story dreamed up by her mother. Jenna didn't understand a diary can be as much a work of fiction as of fact. Or, at the very least, embellished. But then, if her mother and her real father hadn't divorced…?

'Why did your mother go to America?'

'Why, she fell in love, of course.'

'With an American… from Bute?'

'Yes. There was an American Navy submarine base on the Holy Loch and Victor was stationed in Dunoon. Mom said the men posted there would come over to Bute – a change of scene I guess. That's how my mom and Victor met, though I didn't ever get the full story.'

'And your mother took you with her when she ran off to America with Victor?'

'Yes, that's what happened. I was only an infant – I remember nothing about it. I always thought Victor Pattersmain was my dad. You can imagine how I felt when I found out the truth.'

But what was the truth? What's more, I didn't like the gleam in Jenna's eye as she spoke. It should have been a warning she wasn't the meek person I'd first assumed.

She sat back and sighed. 'I'm so pleased to meet up with you again, Alison. From what you told me during the plane journey about how often you've been here, you know Bute well. Why, even from what you've said today, you've already cleared up a problem about the house being near a ferry terminal.'

There was a pause. I'd no idea how to reply, but I'd a bad feeling about what was coming next.

'Will you help me sort this out? I'll make it worth your while.'

The money wasn't tempting, but I can't abide a mystery. I thought again about my computer, about the commission I'd agreed, about Nora's wrath if I didn't meet the deadline. Then again, surely taking a few hours out to help Jenna wouldn't be a problem.

'I'll do what I can,' I said. 'But I'm supposed to be working.'

She looked surprised. 'Gee, really? What are you doing?'

I explained as briefly as I could, and she seemed very taken with the story of Maria North. 'How romantic,' she sighed as I finished. 'To build a village to make sure the woman you loved wouldn't feel homesick.'

'Well,' I hastened on, 'that's the story. I have to find out how much is true.'

It was clear that no matter what I said now, she was determined this romantic account was the one she'd believe.

CHAPTER EIGHT

The first task was to go through the diary carefully, paying close attention to the pages relating to the house on Bute. It was essential to pinpoint accurately the property Jenna thought was rightfully hers.

Problem was, her mother hadn't given a house name and the description could have applied to several properties. Even though I was willing to assist her, I didn't relish the idea of going around randomly knocking on doors. At one time Bute was where wealthy Glasgow merchants built summer houses, an island where they and their families could escape the fetid air of the city. And with the ease of transport by boat direct from the Broomielaw on the river Clyde in the city centre, numerous grand Victorian mansions sprang up.

One thing I was able to confirm: if the house was close by a ferry, and it wasn't near Rothesay, it must be located along the road leading to the Rhubodach to Colintraive crossing. The name of the house was Whinleck and the location was described as 'secluded': a large villa with substantial land around it. Trouble was, there was nowhere of that name on the map, but we agreed there could be a number of reasons for this.

Using the diary and the map of Bute, and fuelled by more coffee, we worked out there were two possibilities. This area of the island wasn't densely populated: there were no more than a few properties dotted about the landscape and most of them were either cottages, probably originally rented to workers, or farms owned by the Mount Stuart estate.

But there were a couple of houses worth investigating: both up past Ardmaleish and Stuck, well-screened from the roadway by trees. The difficulty was neither had the name mentioned in the diary, Whinleck House: the house nearest to the ferry crossing was Phinmore and further along, Cromach Manor.

'The property might have been sold,' I said. 'Your mother's diary was written a while ago. The name of the house could have been changed by the new owners.'

Jenna shook her head. 'No way.' Perhaps she didn't believe this was possible, or she preferred not to think about difficulties that might complicate the search.

'But it does happen,' I insisted. 'New owners, wanting to put their stamp on a property. This was written ages ago. A lot could have happened in the meantime...'

'You don't understand,' she interrupted, 'I'm the rightful owner of this property. Whoever occupies it now, if my dad has passed away, the property belongs to me. He was allowed to live in it for his lifetime...but no more.'

I wasn't about to explain about the Scottish laws of property inheritance, mainly because my own ideas were so sketchy. It wasn't something I'd had to deal with. Instead I stood up saying, 'Take the diary. I'll come along with you to the two houses we think might be worth a visit.' The sooner we did this the better.

It hadn't occurred to her, that though her mother had died, her father might still be alive and I'd no intention of adding to her problems by raising the matter.

'Good idea,' she said and as we left together, 'Do you have a car here on the island?'

'Why, yes. It's parked up in Stuart Street, beside the Bute Museum. The town is so busy today with holidaymakers and I was lucky to find a space.'

She laughed. 'I've hired a car for a couple of weeks, but it freaks me out. It's so tiny and the roads are so narrow. I'd rather you drove, if you don't mind.'

She followed me along the street, through Guildford Square where a lone piper was playing a less-than-cheery tune and up past Rothesay Castle to the Bute museum. She pointed over to a row of cars in the parking bay opposite the Police Station. 'The bright yellow one is mine. Couldn't miss it, could you?'

We walked round into Stuart Street. 'Gee, it's quite a place,' she said, nodding in the direction of the castle. 'I must have photos. It looks pretty ancient.' She pulled out her phone.

'Yes, it was built in the 13th Century and owned by the Stewarts, the hereditary kings of Scotland, through many generations,' I said, then stopped, aware she wasn't paying attention, she was so intent on photographing the castle. The history lesson could wait.

As we approached the car, she went over to the driver's side. 'Oops,' she said, realising her mistake, 'I can't get used to the right-hand drive.'

What with her concerns about the size of her car, the narrowness of the roads and the problem of adjusting to driving on the left-hand side of the road, I was glad we'd agreed to take my car.

One thing did please her. 'I can't get used to how quickly you're able to get about on the island, it's so…so compact.'

I was rapidly beginning to regret my decision to help her, but it was too late now, and we set off, through Rothesay and Ardbeg, to Port Bannatyne, before taking the road leading to the Rhubodach ferry. We drove up towards the Kyles of Bute, Jenna all the while making sounds of admiration at the scenery, except when a stray sheep suddenly jumped out in front of us.

'Gee, what was that,' she gasped, clutching her seatbelt.

'Only a sheep – see, it's decided to re-join the others in the field,' I said.

'It's so pretty here,' she said. 'And so quiet. And look – there are boats on the water.'

I cast a quick glance over. 'Might be a yacht race,' I said, 'judging by the numbers.'

Past the first picnic spot and beyond the old fish farm where the hedgerows were thick with the promise of a good crop of brambles, I pulled into the side of the road to take out the map. 'Cromach Manor, the first possibility, is across there,' I said, 'or at least the entrance to it.'

'We can't drive right up?' She sounded astonished.

'No, look. There's a security gate. We might have to say who we are before we're allowed entry.'

This seemed to annoy her, and she began muttering to herself as she got out of the car. 'Worse than L.A.'

'We can go the rest of the way on foot,' I said, and we walked over to the security gate. But this being Bute, the security gate wasn't locked, and with a gentle push we were able to gain access to the long driveway without having to think up a plausible reason for our visit.

'Gee, what's that awful stench?' she said, wrinkling her nose.

'Only the smell of the countryside,' I said. 'You'd better get used to it.'

As we approached the property, I realised I'd made a mistake, and this couldn't possibly be the house mentioned in the diary. It was too plain, lacking the ornamental façade Jenna's mother had described.

I stopped and grabbed Jenna by the arm. 'This is the wrong place – there's no point in wasting time here.'

She shook me off angrily. 'You said yourself my mom might have disguised some of the details, or not remembered too clearly. Surely it's worth a try.'

She strode ahead and I hurried to catch up with her, worried about how she would approach the owner of this house.

With a confidence I found intimidating, she knocked loudly on the large wooden front door, ignoring the bell-pull at the side.

There was no immediate response and I breathed a sigh of relief. 'Come on, Jenna. There's no one at home.'

But as I turned to leave, the door was suddenly yanked open and we were confronted by a tall, burly man, his bare arms decorated with tattoos.

'Yes,' he growled, rubbing at his eyes. Oh dear! We'd clearly wakened him, and he reminded me of a programme I'd once seen about grizzly bears coming out of hibernation.

I'd let Jenna do the talking… and she did, but her story sounded so muddled I could see him becoming more perplexed with every word she spoke. '…and I've come all the way from California to claim my inheritance.'

Even allowing for the fact she was American, and rather direct in her approach, this was not a good tactic. The man seemed to be taken by surprise, but he recovered quickly as Jenna added, 'Wasn't this house originally called Whinleck?'

'No, it wasn't,' he yawned, now more awake. 'It's been Cromach Manor for as long as I've known it. It's not a family house now: it's been converted into two flats. This is not your inheritance…you've made a mistake.'

That explained the number of cars in the driveway and becoming more and more embarrassed, I tried to drag Jenna away, but she seemed reluctant to give up. 'Are you sure this place wasn't once called Whinleck?'

'Damn sure,' he said, and he banged the door closed.

'That went well,' I said, but Jenna didn't seem to pick up on the sarcasm in my voice.

'He was so rude. You'd have thought he might have been willing to check for us.'

This wasn't what I would have expected him to do. If a stranger turned up at my door, trying to claim my property, I'd have been equally dismissive. It was my fault. I should've briefed Jenna before setting off. And even if this was the right house, as it was now converted into flats, claiming it as her inheritance might prove impossible.

'There's the other house to try, Phinmore House,' she said brightly. 'That must surely be the right one, the one my mom lived in.'

I wasn't nearly as confident as Jenna but had promised myself as soon as we'd visited the other house (though I was certain it would also be disappointing), I'd bid Jenna farewell. I had to get back to the work I was being paid for. This could turn out to be a long chase after a dream of an inheritance, with no certainty of finding out the truth. I'd been under the impression Jenna had been anxious to find her real father. Now it was becoming evident what she was truly interested in was finding a property she might own.

As though on cue, my phone pinged, and I glanced at the screen as we walked back to the car. It was Nora, probably checking up on me and wondering how the commission was progressing. I ignored it. I could deal with this problem later.

Why on earth had I become involved with Jenna? Or rather, with this pursuit of her inheritance? It was the usual story. I couldn't abide a mystery, particularly when there might be a chance I could help solve it. It nagged and nagged at me until I found an answer. And look where it had landed me on previous occasions when I'd visited Bute.

Except, this time, there was no answer and what's more, the story might be no more than fantasy, concocted by Jenna's mother as a way of justifying running off to the United States.

CHAPTER NINE

By now I was certain we'd have no more luck at the next house but, putting aside my doubts, I determined this would be my last contribution to Jenna's quest. We drove through large open wooden gates and crunched up a gravel driveway curving through dense foliage. In this Victorian mansion the builders had certainly gone to town on the embellishment. Wrought iron balconies sat outside the upper-floor windows; the stonework was adorned by strange carvings, several of them fierce-looking creatures bearing no resemblance to any I could identify. Sweeping lawns at the front of the house were interspersed with clusters of azalea bushes and flower beds boasting luxuriant bushes of red and yellow roses, their scent perfuming the air, even at a distance.

This time, we were able to park immediately in front of a few steps leading to the main door. Close up we could see how impressive this mansion was. It was larger than Cromach Manor, its front windows boasted intricate stained-glass panels and the massive oak door was furnished with what appeared to be the original letter box and lion's head knocker. A glimpse of the grounds behind the house showed them stretching away to the boundary of a small orchard.

This time we did use the bell pull at the side of the door, and as we waited for an answer Jenna said, 'Gee, this is quite a place. It must be worth a lot and…' She didn't finish as there was the sound of the front door being unlocked. I was prepared for another testy encounter, so it was a surprise when a wizened woman who scarcely came up to my shoulder appeared. She was leaning heavily on an ornate walking stick.

'Yes?' she said in a whisper, peering round the door.

Jenna stepped forward, preparing to launch into her story about the house but I raised my hand to hold her back. I'd learned a lesson from last time. Trying to explain a complicated story while standing on the doorstep wasn't a good idea and if this was the right house we had to make the most of the opportunity. It might be our only chance.

I said who we were, stressing my credentials as a writer by offering my business card, though by the way she scrutinised it I'd a suspicion she was having difficulty reading it. I didn't mention Jenna's quest. 'Could we possibly come in for a minute?' I said in what I hoped was a persuasive voice.

She looked puzzled, then stood aside to let us pass into the hallway, a vast space with oak panelled walls and a marble floor covered by ancient rugs. If this was Jenna's inheritance, I thought it didn't look too promising, but Jenna appeared overwhelmed, judging by her expression.

The woman stood gazing at us, but there was no invitation to move further into the house.

'Who did you say you are?' So I was right – she had problems with her eyesight.

Before Jenna could answer, I said hurriedly, 'My friend Jenna is here from Los Angeles, trying to trace her family. She thinks she might be related to your family.' I gave a laugh which sounded hollow even to my ears. 'You know what Americans are, how keen they are on finding out where they came from originally, especially if it's Scotland.'

Beside me, I could feel Jenna itching to interrupt, to tell the story about her expected inheritance, but I coughed and gave her a nudge. Far better to use this version of the story. There was no sense in alarming this old lady. Besides, I was still convinced Jenna's story about her inheritance was likely to be no more than that – a story.

'Of course. But I'm not sure how you think we might be connected. I've never heard of American relatives. Come through to the lounge, it's more comfortable there.' She turned to lead us into a large room on the far side of the hallway, all the while leaning heavily on her stick.

'You see,' I hissed to Jenna as we followed her, 'it's better not to rush in with a story about your inheritance, how you think this place should be yours.'

Jenna shrugged, but I could sense she at last agreed with me.

'Sit down, sit down,' the woman said, 'and move Rusty out of the way.'

Rusty was a large golden Labrador, taking up most of the room on the ancient sofa, and he looked most reluctant to move until the woman raised her stick and he jumped down to slink away.

'I wouldn't hit him,' she chuckled, 'but he recognises the signs of authority.'

I would've preferred to stand, given the deposit of hairs Rusty had left on the sofa, but Jenna seemed to have no such qualms.

I introduced myself again and she said, 'I'm Ettie MacDonald. I'm a widow and I live here with my daughter and my son-in-law. Not always a good arrangement for a family but this is a big house, so it works well.'

Beside me, I heard a sudden gasp from Jemma, before she turned it into a cough.

Ettie stopped as though remembering we'd come for a purpose. 'What did you say your friend was called?' She settled herself in the high-backed chair opposite us and folded her hands in her lap, looking at us expectantly.

I repeated the story. 'Jenna is from America and she's trying to trace family she thinks might be here on Bute.'

'Yes,' Jenna said eagerly. 'My mother's name was Kate Pattersmain, and I think she might have lived here at one time.'

A shadow crossed the old woman's face. 'What makes you think we might be related?'

'My mom came from Bute and from her diary, we think this is the house she lived in.'

Luckily Jenna had picked up on the need for discretion and was keeping her answers vague.

But before Ettie could reply, the door burst open and a middle-aged woman came rushing into the room.

'Why, hello, Dana, back so soon. I didn't expect you to return from the mainland till later this afternoon.'

Dana ignored Ettie and frowned at us. 'Who are these people?'

Ettie beamed. 'Some nice people who've come all the way from…where did you say you were from?'

'America,' Jenna said.

'America,' Ettie echoed. 'They think we might be related to them. Isn't it lovely? Their mother lived in this house at one time.'

Before I could stop her, Jenna said, 'My mom was Kate Pattersmain, and her own name was McPharg, and she ran off to America, leaving my dad here, in possession of the house for as long as he lived.' She sat back, an expectant look on her face.

It was almost imperceptible, but there was a change in the atmosphere, a slight pause, before Dana said, 'I don't recall anyone of that name, Pattersmain or McPharg, living here and the house has been in our family for many generations.' She laughed. 'What nonsense.'

'Are you sure?' There was a determination in Jenna's voice. 'Thing is, I don't know much about her time before she married the man who I thought was my dad. I only discovered when mom died the man I believed was my dad wasn't. His name was Foster.'

Dana ignored this complicated story. 'I can't help you. Of course I'm sure we've never heard of either of those names, Pattersmain or McPharg. My father and my mother lived here together all their lives. My father died several years ago. Dana stressed the word 'together' before standing up and saying, 'I'm sorry I can't help you. There's no possibility you could be related to us. It was good to meet you and good luck with your search.'

Why did I not believe her? But it was clear we'd get no more information from her. We'd have to try another tack. As she ushered us out as quickly as possible, Ettie trailed behind, given her need to use the walking stick, and with a peremptory, 'Goodbye,' Dana slammed the door behind us.

I caught the expression on Ettie's face as we left. Something had come back to her, a memory, but there was no way we could ask her, not with Dana standing guard over her.

Jenna looked crestfallen as we made our way slowly back to the car. 'What do we do now? I've clearly made a terrible mistake. My mom was making it up. Why did she do that?'

She looked as if she might burst into tears at any moment.

'Don't despair just yet,' I said thoughtfully. 'That was a little too quick, the way Dana dismissed us. I'm certain she recognised your mother's name.'

Jenna's eyes widened. 'Do you think so? Why would she say she didn't know her?'

'Think about it. You turn up out of the blue, a long-lost relative. She guessed you might have a claim on the estate, if what your mother wrote in the diary was true. Why would she welcome you with open arms?'

'I suppose so,' Jenna said slowly as I started up the engine. 'But who was Ettie then? If she was my father's wife, did that mean my mother and my father were divorced? There would have been a settlement? What will we do now?'

I'd no answer to her questions and I didn't like the use of the word 'we' but in spite of my earlier decision, I didn't want to abandon her completely. Perhaps if I concentrated on research in the mornings, helped Jenna in the afternoons and worked in the evenings, I could finish the commission on Maria North to meet the deadline and keep Nora happy.

51

I dropped her in Guildford Square, and we exchanged phone numbers. 'Leave it with me,' I said. 'I'll give you a call tomorrow – and hopefully we'll have come up with a few ideas by then. The Rothesay library has good archives – we should be able to find what we're looking for there.'

'Thanks, Alison,' she said. 'I do appreciate your help. I realise how stupid it was to come here with no more than the story in an old diary to guide me. I guess I'm so anxious to believe we might have money coming to us…' She didn't finish the sentence. She didn't have to, but the truth was it wouldn't be as simple as she imagined, even if she did have a claim on the property.

I waved farewell as she strode over towards the car park. Now for more important matters: more important to me, that is. I locked the car and began to walk to the computer repair shop, my mind turning to the writing of the commission.

I glanced at my watch. Good. I'd catch the *Speedy Computer Repairs* shop before they closed. My house hunt with Jenna had taken longer than I'd anticipated, and I'd completely forgotten about phoning the shop. But hopefully my there was still time to make a start, if Tyler had worked his magic on my machine.

I'd begin the first chapter by using Baxter's notes, and if I could manage at least a rough draft, I'd feel a great deal better. But when I reached the *Speedy Computer Repairs* shop I saw, to my horror, it was closed. I checked my watch again. No, it was well before closing time. There must be a mistake. I pulled at the door, but it didn't budge. I went up close and shaded my eyes, trying to peer through the window:

no sign of anyone inside. Then I noticed the hand-written sign taped to the side.

Sorry. Due to a sudden family bereavement this shop is closed until further notice.

I took out my phone and called the number underneath the shop sign, but it went immediately to voicemail. Of course, Tyler's phone would be switched off.

This was a setback I couldn't have anticipated. My computer was locked up in this shop. What on earth was I going to do now?

CHAPTER TEN

A quick visit to the café next door provided the reason for the sudden closure of the shop. Tyler's grandfather had died suddenly at lunchtime and Tyler had closed the shop for a couple of days.

The café owner tried to reassure me. 'Don't worry, he'll be back. His granny, as you can imagine, is devastated: it was so sudden. His grandpa had just finished eating his favourite pudding, jam sponge and custard. He loved his food, did old Willie.' She sighed. 'It was the way he'd have wanted to go. As Tyler's their sole relative on the island, he had to dash off to help. Though of course he'll have to take time off for the funeral.'

I didn't mean to be unsympathetic, but I could but hope "a couple of days" meant exactly that. I didn't want to pester him about my computer repair.

'I'll have to wait for him to get in touch,' I said ruefully, before explaining why I was so anxious. With no customers in the shop, she was inclined to chat. 'Mickletean and Son will be arranging the funeral. They seem to have a good reputation.' Her face darkened. 'Though occasionally people think they'll do better by booking a firm of undertakers from the mainland. A lot of nonsense of course.' She sniffed. 'Some people have a high opinion of themselves.'

Not realising there was a hierarchy of undertakers involved, I could do no more than give a half-hearted smile. Several times I tried to finish the conversation, but in the end I resigned myself to listening patiently as she ran through every detail of the last funeral service provided by Mickletean and Son and the high quality of their service. '…and as for Mrs Wilkinson, what a funeral it was. The flowers had to be seen to be believed. Not to mention the meal after the funeral – Mickletean had arranged a special discount and…' I tuned out. I didn't want to appear rude, but the thought crossed my mind she might be entitled to commission for every customer she recruited.

When at last I was able to edge away, I wandered back to Guildford Square, considering what to do next. With this tight deadline, losing two days was a problem. My rough notes were on a computer file, so my decision was to drive over to Kerrycroy in the interim, take as many photos as I could and soak up the atmosphere of the village.

Later I could phone Jenna. If I was to be at a loose end for a couple of days, I might as well use the time to help her find out if there was a grain of truth in the story in her mother's diary.

Once out of town I felt my spirits lift. The afternoon had turned warm and sunny after a misty start. Spending time out of doors would be a pleasure and I'd just have to work twice as hard when my computer was eventually returned to me.

As I drove through Ascog, there were a few children playing on the beach, and once past the old Co-operative Convalescent home, now holiday homes, I spied several seals basking on the rocks.

At the entrance to the village of Kerrycroy, I slid into a space beside the curve of the road leading up to the entrance to the estate of the Gothic mansion that was Mount Stuart House. I hadn't been here for several years and the Kerrycroy houses had had a face-lift, judging by the gleaming paintwork and the neat verges surrounding the properties.

I stood for a few minutes, silently contemplating how deeply the second Marquess of Bute must have loved his wife, Maria, to have this village built for her. And to think she died so young, yet the village remains as part of her legacy. I walked out to the end of the long stone jetty and looked back. A village green fronted a semi-circle of houses and a narrow path and a further expanse of grass mirrored the curve of the beach. Some of the houses were half-timbered in the Tudor style, others were white-washed cottages, each with a little porch. In the middle of the village green stood a large Maypole which looked as if it hadn't been used recently. I tried to imagine how it would once have been, adorned for May Day celebrations, and what had been Maria's reaction to this reminder of home.

So engrossed was I in taking photos of the village, I didn't hear the sound of a car approaching.

'Enjoying your holiday, Mrs Cameron,' a voice said, and I turned suddenly, jumping in surprise to see Tyler from the computer shop opening the door and coming out of a car which had clearly seen better days and had a few bumps, judging by the dents on it. His passenger also got out and stood stretching his arms as though he'd been confined for some time.

'Sorry about your computer,' Tyler said, 'but if you come along to the shop first thing tomorrow morning, I'll be there to let you have it back.'

'You managed to fix it?'

'Good as new,' Tyler said, a wide grin lighting up his face.

Relief coursed through me. Good news indeed to have the computer back earlier than anticipated.

It was then I noticed the well-built man standing beside him was clad in a black suit of material that looked uncomfortable for a day like this. Tyler said, 'Oh, this is Sonny Mickletean. We're heading to my gran's house – Sonny is making the funeral arrangements.'

Sonny gave a little bow and said in a low voice, 'My name is Irwin Mickletean, but people call me Sonny.' He was noticeably sturdy, but his face was long, thin and clean-shaven, revealing front teeth which jutted out and gave him a sullen look.

For a moment I couldn't see the connection, then I said, 'Oh, I see, you're the son in Mickletean and Son.'

'Yes,' he nodded, but didn't elaborate. I should have guessed it was Sonny and not Sunny as I'd first imagined. He wasn't the least bit sunny in disposition, but then this might be the result of his occupation.

Then I remembered why the shop had been closed. Guiltily I said to Tyler, 'Sorry, I should have offered my condolences on the death of your grandfather.'

Tyler dismissed my apology with a wave of his hand. 'No need. It was sudden in the end, but he was almost ninety and had been ill for a long time.'

He nodded to Sonny. 'We should be going.' Then to me, 'I'll see you first thing tomorrow morning.'

They got back in the car and with a toot of the car horn, Tyler and his companion departed, leaving me gazing after them.

I recognised the undertaker and I didn't think it was from a funeral I'd had to attend on Bute. Then I dismissed the encounter from my mind: the good news about my computer overtook other concerns. At last I'd be able to make a proper start on the article about Maria North and the village of Kerrycroy.

In the meantime, I'd make use of the remainder of the afternoon to take more photos. But now, with my computer repaired and a deadline looming, could I afford the time to help Jenna?

CHAPTER ELEVEN

In the end I decided there was no choice about helping Jenna; by now I was intrigued by the story, and the more I thought about it, the more convinced I became there was something strange about Phinmore.

She sounded enthusiastic when I phoned her later to suggest we meet up for dinner. 'That would be great, Alison,' she said. 'I'm pretty much at a loss here – everything is so different from L.A. Where do you think we should go for a meal?'

And Bute is different from the rest of Scotland, I thought, but I didn't say so. 'I'll meet you in Guildford Square at eight o'clock. I'll check if we can make a reservation in Harry Haw's restaurant – it's in the street opposite the Rothesay Castle, so not far, and the food is reliable.'

We were in luck and, reservation made, I went back to the hotel. I'd a couple of hours in hand and besides scrolling through the photos I'd taken during the afternoon, I wanted time to think about the questions I should ask Jenna. Whatever else I might be able to do, I should be able to help her find out the truth. I didn't think there could be any way she was heir to a huge estate and a vast fortune, but perhaps there were relatives on the island who would know the truth about her real father and her trip wouldn't have been entirely wasted.

Harry Haw's was busy, but and they managed to squeeze us into a table in the corner, which was ideal for my plan to discuss the situation with Jenna without being overheard.

'Is it always as crowded as this?' Jenna said, looking round as the waitress came over with the menu. After a few minutes, we settled on fish and chips, hardly an exotic choice, but Jenna claimed she'd '...heard about this popular seaside meal.'

'Look over there,' she whispered, putting the menu in front of her face to hide what she was saying. 'I recognise the guy at the table by the door.'

I followed the direction of her nod. 'Mmm, yes, I've also seen him recently.' It took me only a moment to remember where I'd seen him before. 'Of course. It's Sonny Mickletean. He's the 'Son' in Mickletean and Son Funeral directors. I met him earlier today.' I smiled. 'He looks completely different out of his work clothes.'

And indeed, if it hadn't been for his distinctive front teeth I might not have known him in this outfit of jeans and an open-necked purple shirt.

Almost at the same time as I spoke, Jenna said, 'Oh, that's the guy I met on the ferry.' She lifted her hand to wave at him, saying, 'Hi, there.'

We laughed and Sonny looked up, smiling to acknowledge us, though I wasn't too sure he recognised us.

'I suppose undertakers also have lives,' I said as the waitress arrived with our meal.

As we enjoyed our food, we chatted a bit about life on the island, Jenna showing a gratifying interest in the progress of my commission. But as we debated about dessert, it was time to get down to business.

'I'm willing to help you, Jenna,' I said. 'But I have a limited amount of time. You'll understand from what I've told you this commission will take a lot of work and I need to make use of each minute on this visit to the island. We have to make a plan. We can't go rushing up to another house without agreeing what we're going to say. People on Bute are friendly, but I doubt if any of them would be happy with a stranger turning up and suggesting they should hand over their property.'

She looked crestfallen but she said, 'Guess you've got a point. That kinda makes sense.' She put down her glass of wine with a contented sigh. 'So what do you suggest?'

'We have to do more research before we try other houses,' I said. 'And find out about the last house we visited.' It was my intention to investigate Phinmore first, but this time on my own. I didn't want to give Jenna hope where there might be none. And I was increasingly certain, the more I thought about it, that there was something strange about what had happened there. It wasn't like people in Bute to be so unwelcoming, especially when had Jenna travelled so far to try to find her relatives. But how we'd manage to do this, gain access to the house again, I'd no idea. Ettie knew something, I was certain, but I'd a feeling Dana would be difficult and there'd be little possibility of speaking to Ettie on her own.

Jenna looked puzzled. 'How do we try to find other houses? I thought you said there were only a couple of houses that might be possibles.' She hadn't mentioned Phinmore again and I was glad. I wanted a lot more in the way of hard facts before we made a move. But this was a part of the search I'd be better tackling alone. And I'd a plan for engaging Jenna in something useful.

'The local Library has good records and would be the best place to start. First thing on Monday morning, we'll go there and begin our search. Many of these old houses were renamed over the years as different owners made them their own. If the library can't help they'll be able to tell us where we can try next.' As soon as I'd spoken, I remembered my promise to myself to work in the mornings. Ah, well, one day wouldn't make a difference.

Plan agreed, we paid the bill and left the restaurant. The sun had set by now and the air was cool, the first sprinkling of stars appearing in the night sky. I shivered, wishing I'd brought a warmer jacket.

'Look,' Jenna said, grabbing me by the elbow, 'there's the undertaker again.'

Sonny was standing on the pavement opposite, beside Rothesay Castle. He had his back to us but was instantly recognisable by his purple shirt.

'He looks as if he's on fire,' Jenna said. 'What's all that smoke?'

'Nothing to worry about – it's one of those vaping things. What people use when they're trying to give up smoking.'

'We should go over and say hello properly. He was so pleasant when I met him on the ferry.'

I'd no wish to talk to him and began to walk quickly back to Guildford Square, with Jenna hurrying to keep up with me. 'I'll meet you in Guildford Square on Monday morning at nine o'clock. Don't be late.'

She might want to talk to Sonny, but I'd no intention of doing so.

CHAPTER TWELVE

On Sunday morning I was up and about well before dawn. Despite Tyler's assurances, worries about my computer had kept me awake for a long time the night before. When at last I did drift off, it was to dream of being in a room with a giant computer I couldn't boot up no matter what I tried.

The result was I was standing outside the *Speedy Computer Repairs* shop, in a deserted Rothesay, far too early in the morning. Apart from one or two dog walkers, strolling aimlessly along the prom, there was no sign of activity in the streets. The first ferry of the day was pulling into the harbour and there were stirrings of life in the marina: overnighters wanting to make the most of the fine day it promised to be. I hoped Tyler had remembered what he'd said about opening the shop.

Fifteen minutes later, as I was thinking of phoning to remind him, his battered car screeched to a halt, making me jump in fright.

'Sorry,' he grinned as he got out, 'didn't mean to alarm you.' His hair was still the same bright red colour but had lost its carefully arranged spikiness.

He motioned me to follow him as he unlocked the shop door and switched off the alarm.

'Your computer is through in the back.' He disappeared from view, leaving me standing looking at banks of computers in various states of repair with cables trailing haphazardly off shelves.

He reappeared a moment later. 'Here we are. Good as new. Fixing it was simple really. What had happened was…'

I held up my hand. 'I'm grateful you did this at short notice, Tyler, but there's no point in trying to explain the technicalities to me. As long as it works when I switch it on, that's fine.'

He seemed disappointed at my lack of interest, but he said with a grin, 'Any other problems bring it back. And remember to back up your work.'

Suitably chastened by this reminder, I paid the modest bill and as I was about to leave, he said, 'That friend of yours, the American one, what's she really here for?'

Taken by surprise I said, 'She's come over to look for relatives and check out a property here…' before realising I'd probably given away too much. I rushed on, 'You know what Americans are like about finding Scottish ancestors.'

'Mmm, I heard she'd been up at Phinmore with a tale about her mother having lived there at one time. Don't you think that's odd?'

'You know the people who own the house?' This might be the opening I was after.

'Yes. I helped Dana and her husband set up their new computers.'

'And have they lived there long?'

'Search me,' Tyler said. 'I set up their new computers last year. It was Sonny who told me about your friend visiting Phinmore.'

'So he knows the MacDonalds well?'

Tyler grinned. 'He should. He's married to Dana, Ettie MacDonald's daughter.'

I tried to think of an explanation for Jenna's behaviour: if word got around about her true purpose, we'd not make progress. And this latest piece of news didn't help, so all I said was, 'Thanks again for your help,' and hurried out of the shop before he could ask me more questions.

I'd be meeting Jenna in the morning. I had to talk to her about what we should do next, but should I tell her about Dana and Sonny? Or would this complicate matters further. There was a lot to think about but in the meantime I had to get back to work.

CHAPTER THIRTEEN

Feeling pleased with myself after a day spent researching the story of Maria North, I decided to treat myself to a meal at the Ettrick Bay tearoom. This commission was proving trickier than I'd first imagined and I wondered if Baxter was indeed ill, or if this article had defeated him. I didn't intend to waste time: I printed off the first few pages, taking them with me to edit while I ate.

Maria was a wealthy heiress, but apparently she suffered ill-health and died without producing an heir. Perhaps Kerrycroy was a way the second Marquess hoped to make her feel better – a part of the story I could only guess at without further research. A visit to Mount Stuart archives was called for, and soon, if I was to complete this commission by the deadline.

The tearoom was busy as usual with summer visitors and it looked as if the recently constructed Glamping pods were fully booked. I settled for soup and a toasted sandwich, telling myself it was better to resist the tempting display of cakes sitting in the chill cabinet. I could always return another day.

Lost in thought, at first I didn't notice the young woman who came striding into the tearoom, a teenage girl trudging behind her. It was Dana, so this must be her daughter. When I glanced up, she was busy talking to the waitress and sounds of their laughter drifted across the tearoom. I lifted the pages from my article to hide my face. I wasn't in the mood to meet her, not after our last encounter and I finished my meal as quickly as I could without giving myself a bout of indigestion, then slid out of my seat and went over to pay. By this time Dana had settled at a table in the far corner with her back to me, seemingly occupied by an argument with her daughter.

Once outside, I paused to look over the bay. The water was calm, a distant yacht too far away to make out the detail. The island of Arran loomed large on the horizon, the Sleeping Warrior as it's called, as clear as I'd ever seen it, the tiny island of Inchmarnock dwarfed by its huge bulk. On the beach a family was playing Rounders, the children's screams of delight carrying across the still air. A few brave people had ventured into the water and one was so far out he was but a speck.

Lost in thought, I was startled as 'We meet again, Alison,' a voice said at my elbow. It was Penny Curtis.

'How are you?' I said. 'Are the students enjoying their time on Bute?'

'Absolutely, though it's strange to return after so long. This is the first time I've been back to Ettrick Bay.' She pointed to the crest of the hill on our right-hand side. 'I still have nightmares about that Victorian house, about what happened.'

'You weren't to know,' I said. 'You came over to the island to work on the dig in good faith.'

'Guess so.'

'And I expect your job at Aberdeen keeps you busy?'

'Yes, though I've developed a special interest in genealogy.'

'Really?' This was interesting. 'Is it part of your job?'

'No, it's something I like to do. I've traced as many as I can of my own family and now I'm helping a friend research her ancestry. It's such a big market so if anything goes wrong with the current post, I'll have another career to fall back on.'

I wasn't sure if she was joking, and a glimmer of an idea was beginning to form in my mind, but I had to be careful what I said next.

'Oh, I've a friend who's over from America trying to trace her relatives. She seems convinced there are still several of them here on Bute, but we've had little luck so far.'

'I would've thought with your research skills it would have been quite easy.' I studied her face, but again Penny didn't appear to be joking.

'It's so complicated. I think we need help.'

There was a pause before Penny said, 'I'll help if I can.'

Yes! Exactly what I wanted. I explained about the visit to Phinmore, about our wrong-footing ourselves, but also about my conviction Ettie MacDonald knew more than she was telling us.

At that moment, Dana came out of the tearoom and I sidled round in front of Penny, hoping Dana wouldn't notice me. Penny didn't seem to think this sudden action odd as she continued, 'Why don't you go back, explain it all. Most people are willing to help if they can.'

Trying to think of a plausible reason, I said, 'They may be upset at us coming in and reviving bad memories. Jenna's mother did go off and leave her father.'

A minibus trundled into the car park, disgorging a chattering group of young people.

'Oh, there are my students,' Penny said. 'They've been over at the St Colmac Cottages standing stones, so they'll be ravenous.'

I scrabbled in my bag for one of my business cards. 'Could you possibly give me a call, Penny? I realise you'll be busy with the students on this trip, but if you could spare an hour to go over to Phinmore and ask a few questions, it would be appreciated.'

'Will do,' she said, stuffing the card into the pocket of her jacket before joining the students and her colleagues. She turned to give me a thumbs up as she followed the group into the tearoom. Would this work out?

I hoped she'd remember what I'd said and would be willing to take on the task of visiting Ettie, though yet another person turning up to investigate their ancestry might look suspicious. Even so, it was our best chance. Hopefully Penny would come up with a different idea and anything she discovered would add to the little we already knew.

Back at the hotel I sent a text to Jenna to remind her to be at the library early, but there was no reply and, tired out, I opted for bed. This time it was a dreamless sleep, thank goodness, and I awakened feeling completely refreshed.

CHAPTER FOURTEEN

Penny was true to her word and as I walked up from Guildford Square to meet Jenna at the library, my phone pinged.

Got a free hour this afternoon. Let me have the details and I'll give the family at Phinmore a visit.

This was great news and I felt my spirits lift as I texted back the basic information. I added Jenna's mobile number, in case Penny was unable to contact me. Why I should think Penny could worm the truth from Ettie where we'd failed, I'd little idea, but it was worth a try. In the meantime, I could keep Jenna occupied searching in the library archives. I'd decided once I'd settled her, shown her what to do, I'd leave her in the capable hands of one of the librarians and go back to my room in the hotel to write up what I'd learned so far about Maria North, now determined to keep to my schedule.

Jenna greeted me enthusiastically. 'Gee, Alison, this is so exciting. What do you think we'll find here?'

'I've no idea,' I said, rather taken aback by her jubilant mood. 'It might not be a lot. We have to look through the information available and hope we find clues.'

I didn't recognise the librarian on duty. 'I'm new here,' she said, introducing herself as Val Kinsmore.

'Are you from Bute?'

She shook her head, loosening the clasp holding back a tangle of blonde curls. 'No, my grandmother had a holiday home here, but she died a long time ago. It was no more than a coincidence this post came up at the same time as I decided I wanted out of the city for a while.'

'It's worked out well?'

'I love it here.' Her eyes sparkled as she replied, 'It's so welcoming, you get to know everyone quickly. I feel at home already.'

I explained about Jenna, who'd already found a seat at one of the computers in the room leading to the library and had started scrolling through a microfiche. 'We used these at college, a long time ago. I think I remember how to do it,' she said.

'I'll be glad to help,' Val said. 'Let me sort out these newspapers and then I'll be available.'

She put the front page of one of the dailies in front of me. 'Look, here's the story of poor Yolanda Sperkin, the woman who was killed.'

'Have they found the killer yet?'

'No. Or rather there's been no more word.' She shook her head again, sending the hair clasp dropping to the floor. As she bent to pick it up, she said, 'They thought at first it was an accident, she'd tripped and banged her head. It was at the post-mortem they discovered she couldn't have fallen accidentally.' She shuddered. 'Poor woman…apparently she was a genealogist, had been doing research on the island.'

Yes, I thought, research into Jenna's family. Could there be a connection? Surely not? Yet it did seem a coincidence. If we could find out if Yolanda had left the answer to this riddle on her computer that might help Jenna. There surely must be some notes if she'd been working on it, if she'd emailed Jenna to tell her she'd interesting news for her. What could it be?

CHAPTER FIFTEEN

Jenna must have proof Yolanda had been working for her. The police would be searching the genealogist's computer files, trying to find a clue to discover why she'd been killed. The police would want to interview Jenna and if she explained the situation would she be able to access the information? Very unlikely. We'd have to try a different approach.

In the meantime, I left Jenna happily looking through the archives in Rothesay library though she did say, 'Gee, there's loads here of interest. It's difficult not to get distracted.' At that point she was reading a story about the history of Rothesay Castle and its restoration. 'To think it was once such an important place,' she said, sighing. 'I must take time to visit it properly soon.'

Val was hovering nearby, looking as if she was anxious to be of help, so I'd no qualms about going back to my own research. Returning to write in my hotel room suddenly didn't seem a good idea – I was too restless to settle. Luckily I managed to secure an appointment with the archivist at Mount Stuart to find out more about Maria and check a number of details.

I parked my car on the grass verge and walked across the stone chippings, crunching under my feet, towards the imposing edifice of Mount Stuart House. I entered under the portico to climb the stairs into the main entrance, thinking of the people who had been here before me. It was tempting to dally in the Marble

Hall admiring the splendour of the design and the tapestries adorning the walls, but I was here on business.

The archivist came hurrying down the stairs on the far side to greet me. 'Hello, Alison,' he said. 'I'm Oliver McPhee. You won't remember me, but I was here on a work placement during the time your college group came here for dinner.'

He shook my hand firmly. 'I'm glad you decided to come along to find out about Maria. We have great archives here at Mount Stuart. I'm sure I'll be able to help you.'

I didn't recollect meeting him, but I smiled and nodded, allowing him to interpret my silence as best he could. I didn't want to enter into a discussion about that reunion several years ago…it had caused me a lot of trouble.

'Follow me,' he said. 'There's something I want to show you before we go over to the office.'

He set off quickly and I trotted behind him – Oliver was tall and there was no way I could match his pace.

'Through here. This is the Purple Drawing room and…' he made a dramatic gesture with a sweep of his hand '..this is the portrait of Lady Maria North, who married the second Marquess of Bute. He was supposed to be a pretty dour person, but his wife was well-liked as far as we can tell.'

Often portraits can be of doubtful resemblance to the sitter, but this one struck me as likely to be a faithful rendition.

'She was a wealthy heiress in her own right, one of the three daughters of the Earl of Guilford. Her father settled £40,000 on her when she married – a fortune in those days. And she was due to inherit a third of her father's estates when he died.'

'So he didn't marry her for her money.'

Oliver shook his head. 'I shouldn't think so. The Marquess had property across Britain. He had a great flair for managing the estates, by all accounts. Pity about his eyesight. Goodness knows what he would have achieved if he hadn't contracted an eye condition that left him partially sighted.'

I gazed at Maria's portrait. She seemed to fix me with a steady gaze, her look wistful, perhaps yearning for her native England. Her dark brown hair was fashionably curled, and she wore a simple cream dress and shawl, her single adornment a one-strand gold necklace. I suddenly became aware Oliver was speaking. 'She looks in good health, but in reality she was often ill, and they were a reclusive pair. They spent most of their time here at Mount Stuart. She was said to have greatly missed her native land – hence the building of Kerrycroy.'

'Not a bad place to spend your time,' I said.

Oliver smiled. 'This isn't the original house. There was a terrible fire in 1877 and the third Marquess remodelled the interior, though the chapel and the grand staircase survived.'

'There were no children?'

'No, and she died in 1841. Bute married again four years later – this time his wife, Lady Sophia Rawdon-Hastings and he had an heir at last. It was so important in those days to have a clear succession – else there were so many complications about who should inherit.'

As he spoke I thought of Jenna and the problems she'd become involved in. She certainly wasn't of aristocratic stock, but her mother's actions in running away with an American had caused plenty of difficulties about any inheritance she might have claim to.

'Let's go through to the office. I've looked out various documents, hoping they'll be of interest.'

Grateful as I was, I didn't require a lot of extra material. This was supposed to be an article for general consumption and too much detail would be a hindrance rather than a help. Or, if I was being honest with myself, the trouble was I'd become too engrossed in the research and the article might never be finished.

As we left the main house and walked across the courtyard to the office, my phone rang. Drat! I'd forgotten to put it on silent. I pulled it out of my bag to check it, expecting it to be Jenna reporting what she'd discovered in the library archives. But it wasn't – it was Penny.

'Sorry,' I said to Oliver, 'do you mind if I take this? I'll only be a minute.'

'Not at all. Follow the path round when you've finished. I'll be in the first room on the left.'

'Hello, Penny,' I said. 'Have you managed to find information already?'

'I have, but I'm not sure you'll want to hear this.'

My heart sank. I'd a feeling whatever Penny had found out might make matters worse and I hoped Jenna's trawl of the library's records might have been successful.

'Firstly,' Penny said, 'it took a bit of ingenuity to get to speak to Ettie on her own. Dana was there and the story I gave about doing general research on Victorian houses on the island didn't seem to go down well. I explained I'd a particular interest in what places were called, was writing an academic paper on the ways in which names on Bute had changed over the years, with a special focus on house names, but there was little to be gleaned about a change of name as far as Phinmore is concerned. Dana denied the house ever had another name and as for Ettie…well, I'm afraid her memory is failing her.'

I could see this was going to take longer than I'd first thought. Perhaps I should say I'd ring her back later, but I was eager to hear if she'd made progress. 'And was there anything else?'

She chuckled. 'That's where I had a bit of luck. Someone came to the door and Dana dashed off to open it. Luckily for me, it was a caller intent on having a long conversation, so I slipped in the name of Jenna's mum. "Do you remember a Kate Pattersmain?" I asked her.'

'The only Kate I ever heard of in connection with this house was my husband's first wife, but her surname was MacDonald of course, as mine is.'

'Do you think it could be the same woman?' A bit of me felt I might be grasping at straws.

'Well, I've no idea, Alison. I've no more than the info you gave me.'

'It sounds a strong possibility,' I mused. 'Though MacDonald is not an uncommon name. Did Ettie remember what happened to her, how she ran off to America?'

'But here's the strange thing. She said her husband's first wife died before she met him.'

'She would say that. Probably it's what she was told by her husband to save face, save the embarrassment of admitting his wife deserted him.'

'No. Ettie said Kate had died….and she's buried at the cemetery at Barone, out beyond the High Street in Rothesay. She's even visited the grave.'

CHAPTER SIXTEEN

Stunned by this turn of events, I stood staring at my now silent phone, unsure what to do. Oliver would be waiting for me in the Archives office and I didn't want to disappoint him, given he'd gone to the trouble of looking out material on Maria North.

On the other hand, I was desperate to contact Jenna, question her about this and find out if her trawl of the microfiches in the Rothesay library had yielded anything useful.

It was now mid-afternoon: if I spent a couple of hours in the archives, I could then meet Jenna to catch up. What's more, I need time to think about this latest discovery.

I'd left Penny with the promise I'd phone her as soon as I'd spoken to Jenna. I'd a sneaking suspicion she was now as interested in the problem as I was. I hurried over to the archive office where Oliver was walking up and down impatiently.

'Good, you're here,' he said. 'Let me show you what I've managed to find.'

He lifted the first of the documents with gloved hands and indicated I should pick up the spare gloves on the table. I was glad I'd decided to stay because as I read through letters, notes and household accounts, they made Maria seem more of a real person. Not only did I now have several interesting details to incorporate into this article, with additional work I might have enough for another article on the second Marquess of Bute.

'Would you like a cup of tea?' Oliver asked as I thanked him and made ready to leave, but I declined the offer, anxious to get back to Jenna.

At the look of disappointment on his face, I said, 'It's been such an interesting afternoon and I'd like to come back to do more research on other members of the Stuart family?'

His face brightened. 'Of course. Give me a few days' warning so that I can look out the archives you require.'

I hurried back to my car and drove, faster than I should have, down the driveway and out on to the Mount Stuart road.

Fifteen minutes later, I parked outside the library, hoping I was in time to catch Jenna. But I was too late and as I pushed the door, I realised the library was closed. I knocked on the window, hoping to attract the attention of the librarian who was diligently restoring the children's section to order after a busy day.

Eventually Val looked up and saw me and came over to open the door.

'I'm looking for Jenna,' I said. 'I thought I'd be back before you closed.'

'Oh,' Val said, 'she left about half an hour ago. She had a phone call and went outside to take it. The next thing she apologised for leaving without closing down the microfiche and rushed off.'

'Have you any idea where she went? What the phone call was about?'

I'd no hope Val would know, but I was mistaken. 'I asked if she was okay – she looked shaken when she finished – and she said she'd had an upsetting call from someone called Penny? Would that be right?'

'Yes, sounds like it,' I said. Penny must have phoned Jenna after she'd spoken to me.

'Where did she say she was going?'

'Oh, she said she had to go to the Barone cemetery. I thought this a bit odd, but I didn't want to upset her further.'

'Where is this cemetery?'

'Not far. Continue to the end of the High Street and out of Rothesay. If you keep driving you'll come across it in about a mile down the road. You can't miss it.'

'Thanks,' I said and almost ran to my car, leaving Val staring after me. I was in no doubt she was curious, but I didn't want to tell her about Penny's discovery. I had to get to the Barone cemetery as soon as possible.

CHAPTER SEVENTEEN

The road out of Rothesay was quiet. No matter how often I visited the island, I'd never get used to the lack of a rush hour. And Val was right. The Barone cemetery was easy to find, sitting on the slope of one side of the valley, a quiet and peaceful spot.

I slid the car into a parking space beside Jenna's car at the entrance and jumped out, not bothering to lock it. At first I didn't spot Jenna. She was kneeling down, obscured by a large gravestone adorned with mourning angels and as I approached I could see she'd been crying.

'Oh, Jenna,' I said. 'What's this about?'

She lifted a tear-stained face. 'I don't understand it, Alison. How can this be my mom's grave?'

I came alongside her to look at the inscription.

Katherine McPharg MacDonald
Beloved wife of Foster MacDonald
January 29th 1942 - June 1st 1976
Sleep in peace.

Unable to think of a sensible explanation, I said nothing.

'How can it be? Kate or Katherine, or even MacDonald, isn't an unusual name, but McPharg certainly is. And the date of birth is the same.' Jenna blinked back tears.

This wasn't possible, I thought, then Jenna said, 'I found interesting stuff in the library. Val was helpful, and she managed to find material in old copies of the local paper. Apparently Katherine McPharg MacDonald died suddenly – there was an obituary about how kind she'd been, how her family missed her. And here's her grave. What could be clearer?'

Stranger and stranger.

Jenna stood up and pulled a crumpled piece of paper from her pocket. 'See for yourself.'

I took the paper and smoothed it out. It was a print-off from the local paper, the obituary the librarian had found. There was no doubt about it: the details were clear.

'Do you think my mom was lying? Pretending to be someone she wasn't? I can't think why she would do that?

All I could say was, 'There's no point in waiting here. Let's go back into Rothesay and we can discuss it there.'

She nodded in agreement and with a last lingering look at the gravestone she followed me down to the car parking spaces.

As I was about to open the car door, I stopped. 'We could try Argyll and Bute Council. They might have information. They must keep records of the burials on the island. We can get the death certificate from there.'

Jenna visibly brightened. 'What a good idea. Can we phone them?'

'Not till the morning. The office will be closed now. I suggest we try to meet with Penny. After all, it was a short phone call. There might be something she hasn't told us.'

We drove back to the town, this time at a less reckless pace and luckily Penny was available, "...for a quick coffee. The students are writing up their notes from today". We agreed to meet in The Kettledrum Café at Penny's suggestion. "It's handy for the Glenburn hotel where the students are staying."

She was there waiting as Jenna and I came in, a coffee and large slice of chocolate cake in front of her. 'I didn't have time for lunch,' she said. 'I'm starving.'

Jenna and I settled for coffee. If I kept on eating cake the way I'd been doing the past few days, I'd have to visit The Dressing Room to buy new clothes. Amazing how much cake you can eat without realising it.

'I know you haven't long,' I said. 'But what you told us is difficult to sort out. Jenna's mom died in America, so we're not sure how she can have a grave here.'

Penny's immediate reaction was the same as mine. 'Are you certain it's the same person?'

Jenna nodded. 'The name is the same and the birthdate, though the date of the death of the Katherine McPharg on the gravestone at Barone is 1976.'

'We're going to try Argyll and Bute Council first thing tomorrow morning,' I said. 'They should surely be able to help.'

'Mmm, you would think so.' Penny sounded doubtful. 'I can't suggest a reason for this.'

'Unless…' Jenna hesitated. 'Unless what my mom told me was made up. Is it possible she claimed to be this Kate McPharg, who married someone called MacDonald, even though she wasn't?'

Practical as ever, Penny said, 'But why do that, unless she had a connection to the family?'

'I guess so.' But in the absence of another other explanation, Jenna was clearly clutching at straws.

'Exactly what I said,' I interrupted. 'And why write about it in a diary she didn't think anyone would read?'

Jenna ignored me. 'Maybe she wanted me to have an inheritance, knew of these people, the Mc Phargs who owned Whinleck House, and the mother Katherine McPharg, who'd married a MacDonald…'

Penny held up a hand. 'Stop there, Jenna. Don't you think this is highly unlikely?' She looked across at me, and I nodded in confirmation.

'Besides,' I repeated, 'you said your mother didn't expect the notebook would ever be read by anyone. It was a kind of secret diary. So what would be the point of concocting this elaborate plot?'

'No idea,' Jenna said, 'but do you have a better explanation?'

Her question silenced both me and Penny and we concentrated on drinking our coffee. We'd reached a stalemate and there was nothing else to be done until the Council offices opened in the morning.

'Wait a minute,' I said. 'Do you remember the exact date of the death of Katherine on the gravestone at Barone?'

Jenna nodded. 'I took a photo on my phone.' She reached down into her bag and pulled out her phone to scroll through her gallery of photos. 'Here it is. 1st June 1976.'

'And do you have the entry in the diary? The one telling when your mother left for America?'

'Yep…it's here somewhere. Give me a minute. Here it is.'

She passed the diary to me and I laid it on the table side by side with the phone: I looked at the date her mother had left for America and then at the date on the gravestone. They were identical.

CHAPTER EIGHTEEN

If the Council employee on the other end of the phone seemed surprised by our garbled request, he was unfailingly polite. 'I can check for you, if you can hold on.'

Jenna and I were using the phone in my hotel room on speakerphone. Although he was gone only a short time, it seemed ages. When he did return it was with the news we expected.

'Yes, I have the death recorded as you said. Do you want to purchase a copy of the certificate?'

Jenna nodded. 'That would be good,' I said and paid, thanking him for his help.

'I don't know what good it will do to have the certificate,' Jenna said.

'Oh, there will be useful details on it,' I said. 'Including who registered the death. It might give us a clue.'

She didn't look convinced. 'I guess this will take a day or two to arrive,' she said. 'What will we do in the meantime?'

I thought for a minute, knowing how anxious she was to make progress. I was also eager to make progress – with the article I'd been commissioned to write. My plan of dividing up the day to allocate enough time to this task was rapidly falling apart.

'What about Yolanda's computer? There might be data there, something she'd discovered for you.'

Jenna shook her head. 'I tried that, but it's evidence in a murder enquiry so nothing will be released meantime.'

'There is one other thing we could do,' I said hesitantly. 'We could check the undertakers. They might have more information.'

'Such as?' Jenna remained doubtful.

'They would have prepared the body for burial,' I said. Truthfully, this search for a missing inheritance was becoming gruesome as well as time-consuming. 'There must be documentation relating to this Katherine McPharg MacDonald in their records.'

'Let's give them a call, then.' Jenna visibly brightened at this suggestion.

'The only undertaker on the island is Mickletean and Son as far as I know…'

'Oh, the guy I met on the ferry. He'll be helpful, I'm sure.'

'I don't think he would have organised the burial – he's too young. It must have been his father who dealt with it, but we could contact Sonny first as we've already met him.' I didn't tell Jenna that Sonny was married to Dana – this was a different line of enquiry we were pursuing.

We'd met him only briefly, but this was as good a place to start as any and I checked out the number for Mickletean and Son and dialled it.

The phone was answered immediately by Sonny himself. 'The girl who answers the calls is off sick,' he said. 'We're finding it impossible to manage. I don't suppose you know someone who would fill in?'

'Can't say I do,' I answered more abruptly than intended, then told him what we were trying to find out, giving Katherine's full name and dates.

There was a long silence and I thought we'd been cut off.

'Hello, hello, are you still there?' I said.

'Yes, yes, but I wouldn't have been involved. I only joined the firm ten years ago. My dad would have organised the funeral.'

'Can we speak to him? Or can you check?'

'Well, it's not as easy as you think. A lot of the early records were lost. What's more, my dad's been having problems with his memory for some time and I'm in charge.'

Ah, so Mickletean and Son was Sonny on his own. No wonder he sounded stressed.

'But we could speak to him?'

'I don't know what help he'll be able to give you. He's in the Hereuse Nursing Home at Ascog. He's been there for a while and I don't expect he'll be returning home.'

'But we can visit him?' He might not be as forgetful as Sonny was trying to imply.

'It won't do any good.' Sonny's attempt to put me off only made me more determined.

'I think we'll give it a try. We won't stay long and the smallest thing he can remember would be helpful. We're at a loss with this problem.'

I'd given Sonny the vaguest of details, hadn't mentioned Jenna's desire to claim her inheritance, but he sounded suspicious. I could do no more than guess Dana had told him about our visit.

'Why would you want to go to the Hereuse to see my dad? I've told you he can't help.' He became increasingly angry. 'I don't want you to go there and upset him. He's in a fragile state. You'll make matters worse.'

'We'll be very careful,' I said as calmly as I could in the face of this outburst, though I was becoming more convinced there must be a good reason why Sonny wanted to discourage us from making a visit. 'If it looks as if your father is the least bit distressed, we'll leave.'

'If you must go, make sure you don't upset him. I'll phone the Nursing home and let them know you're coming. I'll be there to join you as soon as I can. Wait till I check the diary.'

I had to agree to this arrangement, albeit reluctantly, as we'd lose the element of surprise. But to be honest, I'd little hope Mickletean senior would be of assistance and if his memory had deteriorated as badly as Sonny claimed, he was unlikely to be able to remember events from over forty years ago. Still, it was worth a try in the present circumstances.

We waited in silence, listening to the tinny sound of *My Way* before Sonny came back to us, saying grudgingly, 'I can't do a meeting today. I have a funeral at eleven and another one at two. The earliest I can manage is tomorrow afternoon. I could meet you at the Hereuse about two o'clock.'

'That would be fine,' I said, as Jenna nodded in agreement.

'And we can't stay long,' he warned as a parting shot. 'Half an hour at the most. My father tires easily.'

While it was good to know he was so concerned about his father, this was a lead we had to follow, and I rang off confirming our plan to meet at the nursing home at two o'clock the next day.

'Do you think his father will be able to remember what happened?' Jenna said.

'I'm not sure,' I said, 'but I've almost run out of ideas. If he can't help us, you may have to abandon thoughts of trying to find your inheritance, unless you want to engage a lawyer.'

Jenna shuddered. 'With no guarantee of success? I don't have the money for that.'

I said, 'In that case, what I do suggest is we go along a bit earlier than suggested to meet Sonny's dad. I've a feeling Sonny's presence might be a hindrance.'

She nodded again. 'I'm not giving up – not yet,' she replied fiercely. Then her tone softened. 'I do appreciate everything you're doing for me, Alison. But I'm sure my mom was right and there is an answer to this – I just don't know what it is yet.' Then she smiled. 'There's time before we meet up with Sonny, and before the death certificate comes through. What do you suggest we do in the meantime?'

I knew exactly what I should be doing, as I reflected on the amount of work still needed to finish my article.

CHAPTER NINETEEN

As Jenna and I drove over to visit Sonny's father after lunch the next day, I tried to put all thoughts of my earlier visits here out of my mind. A large pair of wrought iron gates stood at the entrance, with the name of the Hereuse Nursing Home on a large sign at the front, but as we drove up to the main building I realised how different it was. Many of the trees which had once lined the road had disappeared, leaving an impression of lightness. And the large Victorian villa had been spruced up, the stonework cleaned, and new windows and doors installed.

Inside reflected the outside changes. The hallway, serving as the Reception, was painted in restful shades of cream and white with light wood furniture instead of the massive desk which had once dominated the space.

We rang the bell on the counter to announce our arrival and a young woman, dressed informally, came forward to greet us.

I explained the purpose of our visit – at least I said we were here to visit Sonny's dad.

'Ah, yes,' she said. 'Crawford Mickletean. Sonny said you'd be coming over. He's in the front lounge. He'll be delighted to have visitors, though I must warn you, occasionally in the middle of speaking, he drifts off.'

'We won't stay too long,' I said as we followed her through to an airy front room. In the far corner a quartet of elderly ladies were playing cards and a large table in the centre appeared to be a hive of activity under the direction of a sparky young woman.

'We like to make sure the residents keep busy,' the young woman said. 'And here's Crawford.'

He was sitting in a chair by the window and wasn't what I'd expected. Where Sonny was burly, Crawford was small and thin, sunk deep in his wingback chair. A zimmer stood beside him within easy reach.

'Visitors for you,' the young woman said, leaning over and raising her voice.

'Stuff and nonsense,' Crawford said without turning around.

This didn't look like a promising start. The young woman smiled. 'Don't worry. Take it slowly.' She indicated a couple of chairs beside the window and Jenna and I sat down.

'I'll come back in half an hour,' she said.

Crawford moved his head slightly and stared at us. 'What do you want?' he mumbled.

There seemed no point in wasting time on formalities. 'I wanted to ask you about a funeral you conducted,' I began, but he interrupted, 'I don't do funerals now. You'll have to find another undertaker.'

'No, no,' Jenna said. 'This funeral was over forty years ago: Katherine or Kate McPharg MacDonald.'

A blank look was the answer to this.

'It's no use. We're wasting our time,' I muttered to Jenna.

Suddenly Crawford sprang to life, struggling to rise from his chair. 'Why do you want to know about that,' he shouted. 'It's over and done with. She's dead and buried. Why bring it up again…'

Alarmed by the noise, the young woman came rushing in. 'Now, now, don't get upset,' she said to him. 'Let's get you settled back in your chair.' She motioned to us to leave, saying in a whisper, 'There's no point in waiting when he's like this. From time to time old memories disturb him.'

We slipped out quietly and looking back I saw the young woman talking soothingly to him as he gradually calmed down.

Once back in the car, I noticed Jenna was trembling. 'How awful,' she said.

'Sonny did warn us. It looks as if he doesn't want to be reminded of the past. This is a close community where most people know one another. And it's possible he knew this Katherine well.' I didn't add, that's why Sonny didn't want us to go on our own.

Jenna slumped into the passenger seat and we drove back in silence to Rothesay. I was glad we'd left the nursing home before Sonny's arrival. 'I have to work on my article,' I said, as I dropped her off at her hotel. 'I'll be in touch later.'

She shrugged and got out of the car without a word. Jenna might be upset, but there was nothing more to be done. I was out of ideas and my hope now was that Jenna would decide her quest was fruitless and go back home early.

I couldn't settle. I switched on my laptop and sat staring at the screen, then typed a sentence or two before rereading what I'd written. It wasn't particularly inspiring, and I didn't think Nora would be happy with what I had. Thoughts about Jenna and her family mystery kept going through my head. Why would Jenna's mother assume a false identity? Or think she'd a claim to the Phinmore Estate? If indeed it was the right estate? And the police seemed to be making little progress in finding Yolanda Sperkin's killer. What's more the genealogist's death might have nothing to do with Jenna's family search. I was seriously out of ideas about what to do next.

I gazed out of the window. A solution might be to move my laptop away from the distraction of the view across the water. But this wasn't the problem and I forced myself to check my latest notes and complete another paragraph.

There was a knock on the door and Izzie came in. 'How are you? We haven't seen much of you here?'

'No,' I agreed. 'I've been out a lot.' Then I had a flash of inspiration. 'How long have you lived here, Izzie?'

'Forever, or so it seems,' she laughed. 'All my life except for a couple of years when I worked on the mainland. I couldn't wait to come back.'

'What do you know about Phinmore House, the place on the way to Rhubodach?' I described where it was.

She frowned. 'Oh, you mean the house at Phinmore. Not a great deal, though I've heard people say the family keep themselves very private. They don't socialise. But perhaps it's because the son-in-law is an undertaker. Might spook some people. Why do you ask?'

I didn't want to fuel island gossip, so I said, 'Oh, a friend of mine was interested in the house.'

'I don't think they'll sell it,' she said.

If she thought that was why Jenna here, so much the better. I didn't contradict her, and she left saying,

'Remember, if you need anything you only have to ask.'

Slowly but surely I became immersed once more in the story of Maria North till the sound of my phone startled me.

I glanced at the screen. It was Jenna and I hesitated before answering it.

'Hello, Jenna,' I said, expecting she was at a loose end and looking for company. I was wrong: she sounded so excited I could hardly make out what she was saying.

'Wait, wait, slow down,' I said.

'I've had the death certificate through,' she said.

'And?'

'The name's the same as my mom's and the dates check out but here's the thing. The address is registered as Whinleck House, Phinmore.'

I felt a shiver of excitement. 'Sounds promising,' I said cautiously.

'There's more.' She paused. 'The person who registered the death was Ettie.'

CHAPTER TWENTY

This discovery cast a whole new light on the search. Not only did it now appear the original name of the house was Whinleck as mentioned in the diary, but Ettie had registered the death of Katherine McPharg MacDonald. She couldn't have failed to recognise the name when Jenna mentioned it. And the only possible reason was that Ettie and Foster had never married.

Jenna's elation at finding this piece of the jigsaw was understandable and it was several minutes before she calmed down. 'It's a cover up,' she said. 'The family wanted my mom declared dead, so there would be no question of the estate passing to me once my father died. I'm going back over there right now. That daughter of Ettie's, Dana, must have something to do with it. I knew Ettie wasn't as forgetful as she wanted us to believe.'

'Wait, Jenna. You can't go rushing in there accusing the family of pretending your mother was dead.'

'I've come all this way,' she said, her voice rising with excitement. 'I intend to sort it out. I will have what's mine, what's my right.'

She cut off the call, leaving me confused. Should I go over to Whinleck to give her support, or let her sort this problem out on her own? In the end conscience won. She'd need a witness to any discussions and what difference would another couple of hours make?

I saved what I'd written, closed down the computer and grabbing my bag, I hurried out to my car. The afternoon had clouded over, and a few spots of rain spattered the windscreen as I drove through Rothesay, but I couldn't waste time going back to find a brolly.

What would happen now? If she did as she said, confronted the family, determined to tell them her mother and her father had never divorced, to prove she owned Whinleck House, there was no question what the next step would have to be. Jenna would have to find a lawyer: this was too complicated for someone with little knowledge of the law. The result would be delays and costs with no guarantee of the outcome she wanted.

I sped up as I reached the end of Port Bannatyne village, narrowly missing a tractor heading down from Ettrick Bay and arrived at Phinmore in record time. I'd sent a text to Jenna before leaving, telling her to wait for me but there had been no reply and my phone lay on the seat beside me. She must be busy talking to Ettie, or more likely, to Dana.

By now I was convinced Dana was at the bottom of this scam. I remembered about Yolanda, the genealogist, and a terrible thought occurred to me. Was Dana involved in Yolanda's death? Had Yolanda turned up asking questions about the estate had Dana seen her inheritance disappearing? If so, Jenna was in danger. How I wished I'd left a message at the hotel to say where I was going.

It wasn't too late. I pulled off the road at the bottom of the driveway, aware I was using up precious minutes, but for once common sense told me not to rush into a difficult situation. I rang the hotel number, but there was no reply. Of course, at this time in the afternoon, with guests busy on their various activities, Izzie would most likely be out. I left a message, reckoning it was better than nothing, as with an increasing sense of anxiety I started up the car again and drove up to the main door of Phinmore House.

All was quiet and peaceful. There was no sign of life, nor of Jenna's car, which was strange. I was sure she'd said she was coming straight over. Perhaps she'd parked it round the back of the house. I jumped out of the car and ran up the few steps to ring the bell insistently.

There was the sound of footsteps and then the door was yanked open. Dana stood there, frowning. 'Yes? What is it?'

I hadn't thought what story I might give her, so sure was I Jenna would be there. 'I'm looking for Jenna,' I said. 'She told me she was coming over.'

Dana appeared genuinely puzzled. 'Jenna? Why would she come over here? We cleared up the story about her mother being a relative last time you were here. There's nothing more to be said, so why would she come back?'

Trying to play for time, I said, 'Are you certain? She was so excited; said she'd found new evidence…'

I stopped as Dana glowered at me. 'She's not here, I tell you.' She peered out into the front of the driveway. 'And you can see for yourself her car's not here: it's not possible to miss that bright yellow monstrosity. How would she manage to get out here without transport.'

I was at a loss what to say next. Best to call it a day. For whatever reason, Jenna had decided against coming to Phinmore House. I knew she worried about driving a small car on what were to her narrow roads, or she might have been wary of arriving here on her own. Now I was angry. She might at least have replied to my text; told me she'd changed her mind. I felt rather foolish, standing there arguing with Dana. It was clear Jenna's car was nowhere around.

'Sorry to have bothered you,' I mumbled. I was having no more to do with this search. Jenna could sort it out for herself.

As I turned away embarrassed and smarting from the thought of a wasted journey, I could sense Dana standing there at the front door gazing after me. No doubt she wanted to make certain I left. Well, she could be assured I'd never again set foot on the Phinmore estate and I'd have no hesitation in telling Jenna why.

But suddenly I stopped and turned back. Dana was still standing there motionless, her face a mask.

'What is it now?' she said.

How could I have been so stupid. 'How would you know Jenna's car wasn't here? What it looked like? When we came here before, we used my car. Jenna doesn't feel confident driving on the roads here.'

There was a pause and for a minute I thought Dana was going to slam the door in my face.

Instead she stepped forward and said, 'There's a perfectly simple explanation for this. Why don't you come inside, and we can talk about it. I'm sure we can sort out this misunderstanding.'

Why did I agree? It was a big mistake.

CHAPTER TWENTY-ONE

As soon as the main door closed behind me, I felt a surge of fear. What if there wasn't "a perfectly simple explanation"?

Dana propelled me through to the lounge, her hand firmly on my back. 'Sit down,' she said, pushing me into a chair. 'You can join your friend.'

Jenna was sitting in the chair opposite, and when she saw me and heard Dana's words, a look of terror came over her face.

'This is ridiculous,' I blustered. 'What's going on?'

'I came over to confront Dana, tell her what I know, and she invited me in,' Jenna whispered.

'I didn't see your car.'

'No, Dana told me to park it round the back of the house, next to the old stables.'

Dana went over and stood in the doorway, blocking our exit, as though trying to decide what to do next. 'Why couldn't you leave well alone, Jenna,' she hissed. 'What did the estate matter to you?'

In spite of her fear, Jenna said, 'Because this place is mine. I need it, need the money.'

Dana laughed. 'Of course it's not yours. Your mother abandoned it, abandoned her husband, ran off with some Yank from the base at Dunoon. That's as good a way of handing over a place as any. My dad died a few years ago and my mother is the owner – I'll inherit it when she dies.'

While she was talking, I looked all around the room, seeking a way of escape and raising the alarm. It should be easy if I could signal my intention to Jenna. Sadly she was too engrossed in arguing with Dana to pay attention to me.

Jenna shook her head. 'If you know my mom went to America, what's this business about a grave out at the cemetery at Barone?'

Dana went pale and I realised she'd given herself away.

Taking advantage of Dana's discomfiture, Jenna went on regardless as I tried to signal she should say no more. Dana couldn't have hopes of keeping us in the house for long. She must have another plan…problem was, I didn't know what it might be.

'Yolanda came here, didn't she? Then you understood there might be a difficulty for you.' She paused. 'And why you changed the name of the house, wasn't it? Easy to do, interchange Whinleck and Phinmore. Why didn't I pick up on this earlier?'

'Think you're clever, don't you – you and that genealogist.'

Jenna looked as if she was about to speak again, then stopped as awareness dawned. 'You were responsible for her death, weren't you? You killed her.'

Dana shrank back as though she'd been struck. 'No, no,' she shouted. 'I didn't kill her.'

'But she came here?' Jenna stood up.

'Yes. Nosing around, asking all kinds of questions about the estate, about the inheritance. We tried to put her off, but nothing would work. She said she was going to tell you the whole story. We couldn't let that happen.'

Now was the moment to act. I sprang to my feet, leaned over and grabbed an astonished Jenna by the arm. If we used every bit of our strength, Dana would be no match for the two of us. 'Let's get out of here. There's no way she can keep us.'

I pushed past Dana. 'It's all over for you and your family. We're going straight to the police – you can expect a visit from them very soon. And Jenna will be able to prove she should inherit. Time's up.'

I must say I felt rather pleased with myself. The mystery was solved, Jenna could set in train the legal procedures for claiming the Whinleck estate and I could get on with finishing my article at last.

'I don't think so, Alison,' said a voice and I found our exit blocked by the bulk of Sonny Mickletean.

CHAPTER TWENTY-TWO

The look on Sonny's face didn't inspire me with confidence we'd be out of here soon. A dozen scenarios went through my head, none of them good.

'Go through to the boot room and bring the coil of rope on the bench,' Sonny said to Dana.

As she stood as though rooted to the spot, again he yelled. 'Get the rope, Dana.'

I hoped the rope was to tie us up, though that would be bad enough. After a slight hesitation, Dana ran out of the room, presumably to do his bidding. Was it worthwhile trying to rush him? I couldn't do it on my own and after a show of bravery, Jenna had lapsed back into a state of terror, collapsing into the chair.

'What are you going to do with us?' I said.

He glared at me and it was then I understood he'd no idea what to do next. This was as far as he'd managed to plan.

'Shut up,' he said, then added, 'There are plenty of places on the estate where we can put you and you'll never be found.'

He said this with an air of bravado that made me suspect we'd caught him off guard and he wasn't as organised as he was trying to make us believe.

'It wasn't Dana who killed Yolanda, it was you?' How could I have failed to see?

'It was an accident! She found out the truth about the inheritance, that your mother and my father had never divorced. I went to reason with her, persuade her to stop, ask her to tell that stupid American,' he pointed at Jenna, 'she was mistaken. At this distance it would have been so easy, and I'd have made it worth her while. She laughed at me – can you believe it? Laughed at me and said finding the truth was more important than money.' He rubbed his jaw. 'I couldn't let it happen. I meant to frighten her, show her I meant business. I wasn't to know she'd lose her footing, fall and crack her head. Underneath the carpets on those old cottages, the floors are stone.'

For a moment he looked distraught, then seemed to recollect himself. 'And now there's the problem of getting rid of you two.'

'You could let us go,' Jenna said, with a tremble in her voice. 'I'll forget about the inheritance, go back to the States at once.'

Sonny shook his head and pointed to me. 'You might, but there's no way I could trust her. She's well-known for poking her nose into other people's business, things of no concern to her.'

While I felt hurt by this assertion, I had to admit there was a little truth in it, so I tactfully said nothing. No use in upsetting him more. I needed time to think.

'But you owe us the answer to one question,' I said. 'What's the story of the 'death' of Jenna's mother?'

A look of cunning came over his face. 'Oh, there was a great idea. All dad had to do was accept the death certificate and provide a coffin. Easy when you're the firm of undertakers making the arrangements and conducting the funeral.'

'But surely a doctor would have had to sign a death certificate?' Let him have a response to that.

Sonny made a face. 'You've been to the Hereuse Nursing Home. Dad used to visit an old doctor he knew there. Easy, really.'

'You mean…you mean…' Jenna said, 'the grave up at Barone cemetery is empty.'

'Of course …there is a coffin with several large stones in it, to give the feeling of the weight of a body…'

'But why?' I interrupted.

He whirled round to face me. 'When Ettie dies, Dana and I will inherit, but it might be a long time off. You can see she's in rude health. In the meantime, I have to make a success of the funeral business. You saw my father – he's not been able to work for a number of years. Have you the slightest idea how much the Hereuse Nursing Home costs?'

'You're in debt? You've borrowed on the strength of inheriting the estate.'

He ignored me. 'Where is she? What's taking her so long?'

I persisted. 'But you're the only firm of undertakers on the island – you must make a reasonable living?'

He gave a hollow laugh. 'What do you know? Have a look at the gravestones in the cemeteries on Bute. People here live long. There's not enough business to keep us solvent. And we've a good reputation. Why should I suffer because of what my dad did?'

He moved about restlessly. 'Where the hell is she?'

If I could distract him while his back was turned, we might manage to escape. There were two of us and only one of him and the element of surprise would help. I made a sign to Jenna and she nodded in understanding of my intention.

But we were too slow and as I lunged forward, Sonny spied what we were doing. 'Oh, no, you don't,' he said, putting out his foot and tripping me up, and I fell headlong on the carpet. Jenna should have taken the opportunity to make a run for it, but she seemed frozen by this development.

That was it. Dana would be back at any minute and once we were tied up, there would be no escape.

There was a movement at the door. 'At last. What kept you, Dana?' Sonny growled, keeping us firmly in view.

Dana came in, but she was being pushed into the room by a burly police officer, closely followed by Izzie from the hotel.

'What…' Sonny whirled round, realisation dawning as another couple of policemen entered and grabbed him.

Izzie chewed her fingernail. 'When I got your message, Alison, I remembered what you'd asked me about the house at Phinmore. And I've lived on the island my entire life. I wondered why the name would have been changed, the house called Phinmore instead of Whinleck at Phinmore. Besides,' she looked at me sheepishly, 'you always seem to be in trouble when you come here so I phoned the police. At first they thought I was making a fuss about nothing, but I reminded them of other times you've been on the island and needed help.'

What could I say except a sincere thanks?

I turned to Jenna, who was sitting in the chair by the window, relief written all over her face. 'It's up to you now, Jenna, to sort out the inheritance problem,' I said. 'I've an article to write.'

EPILOGUE

Jenna decided to stay on for a while to begin the process of claiming the estate. There were plenty of loose ends to tie up, including Ettie's involvement in the fraud. After all, she'd been the one who registered the 'death' of Katherine McPharg MacDonald.

'I've found a great lawyer,' Jenna told me when I phoned her from Glasgow. 'And I'm not sure if it might not be better to sell up in the States and come to live here. Though persuading Ulmer might be difficult.' She appeared satisfied she was on the way to being the owner of Phinmore, or rather Whinleck. Keeping the house might be the better option. I wasn't quite sure if she sold the estate she would be as rich as she imagined. The house had been sadly neglected over the years and the site wasn't one to appeal to a developer on Bute. I'd done what I could and made certain she contacted Penny to thank her. Without her help, we might never have managed to solve the mystery.

While I was pleased it had worked out well for her, I was cross with myself for being so eager to become involved. Not simply because once again I'd put myself in danger, but because I was now left with little time to finish the article. I'd have to make do with the material I'd gathered and my photos of Kerrycroy.

I saw Jenna for the last time a few weeks later. She called me from the airport hotel, the night before her flight left for LA. 'Please come over and have dinner with me,' she said. 'It's the least I can do given the help you were in tracking down my inheritance. I'm going back to the States for a while.' She laughed. 'I'll have to find a way to persuade Ulmer to come back to Bute with me. I'm sure once he sees Whinleck for himself, he'll be blown away.'

It was a good way of putting an end to the story and I agreed to meet her in the restaurant of the airport hotel. I wanted to find out if her plans to keep the house were no more than a pipe dream.

'And is everything on the way to being settled?' I asked.

'Not quite. There's a lot to sort out, but I've confidence in the attorney, I mean the lawyer, I've hired. She seems to think there's plenty of evidence to back up my claim.' She sat back and sighed. 'I'll be so pleased to get home. Ulmer is delighted with the news. If I can't persuade him to come over here, then once the estate is sold, it'll give us a fresh start.'

Ah, so perhaps she was already wavering about taking up residence on Bute.

I'd no intention of continuing to keep in touch with her, apart from perhaps a Christmas card, but we said goodbye with a feeling of affection, after all we'd been through together.

'You did well, Alison,' Nora said approvingly, when I went to see her the next day. I'd managed to make the deadline – just – and was concerned the article might not meet her exacting standards.

'Yes,' Nora said. 'You're clearly good at this kind of historical writing. Though I guess being able to work in the peace and quiet of the Isle of Bute was a great advantage. None of the distractions of the city.'

I said nothing. If only she knew.

THE ISLE OF BUTE MYSTERY SERIES

The House at Ettrick Bay: An unexpected discovery at an archaeological site leads to murder.

Last Ferry to Bute: Mysterious deaths at a nursing home and a shady antiques dealer.

Last Dance at the Rothesay Pavilion: Past events cast a long shadow over the present.

Endgame at Port Bannatyne: The world of filmmaking hides a deadly secret.

Grave Matters at St Blane's: A proposal to build a theme park is the catalyst for violent events.

Death at the Kyles of Bute: The Kyles Hydro Hotel is re-opened, with deadly consequences.

Bad Blood at Rothesay Castle: Danger awaits Alison Cameron on her latest assignment.

Deadly Secrets at the Standing Stones: A surprise announcement leads to murder.

*

The Isle of Bute Mystery series: Prequel

When Old Ghosts Meet: Dangerous events are sparked off by a chance sighting on the Edinburgh to Glasgow train.

*

The Isle of Bute Mystery Series: Novellas

Susie's Story: How Susie came to inherit the house at Ettrick Bay.

Dark Deeds at Bute Noir: A crime writing festival with a real killer on the loose.

Decision Day at Kilmachal: A Christmas wedding is not what it seems.

Acknowledgements

Many thanks to Bill Daly and to Joan Fleming for reading the manuscript and for making helpful comments.

Also to Sandra Blair Cobain for advice on obtaining documents (any errors are my own).

And as always, thanks to Paul Duffy of Brandanii Archaeology and Heritage (www.discoverbutearchaeology.co.uk) for technical assistance and for answering my queries.

44324519R00073

Printed in Poland
by Amazon Fulfillment
Poland Sp. z o.o., Wrocław